# Crossing Magic

## By

## Roxanne Capaul

# Table of Contents

*This book is dedicated to my sweet friend*

*Lisah Runninghorse*

*May her gentle spirit forever run free*

*In the afterlife, there are super beings*

*that only exist on Plane 6.*

*Their job is to transition humans who*

*have chosen otherworldly methods to keep them alive*

*past their universal death due date and time.*

*These Earthly humans become Class X Recoveries.*

*Plane 6 Elites bring them home.*

# Afterlife Plane Levels

**PLANE 1:** Evil and otherworldly beings and entities inhabit this level. There are no human souls or any other Earthly species here.

**PLANE 2:** All species that have committed crimes or require special debriefing remain here until they have been absolved and can move on to Plane 3.

**PLANE 3:** This is where the majority of human souls and all other species ultimately live together in harmony.

**PLANE 4:** All basic recovery/transition training takes place here. These souls can travel between Planes 3 and 4. They live on Plane 3.

**PLANE 5:** Class X Recovery training occurs here, and these souls have been through basic recovery training. They live on Plane 3, and interact with visiting Plane 6 Elites while in training on this Plane. Crossovers of all species and humans are overseen by The Ancients.

**PLANE 6:** Only Plane 6 Elites live on this plane along with animal souls and other nonhuman species of their choosing. They perform Class X Recoveries and are under the watchful eye of the Creator.

**Master Plane:** The Creator dwells here with the Supreme Beings, Ancients and other enlightened beings, angels, and guides.

# Chapter One

A gentle breeze flowed through the pristine, white linen curtains that seemed to gently form walls around the ethereal palace that is the office of the highest order of Plane 5. Looking down the long, black marble hallway ahead of him, Levi marveled at the massive white pillars looming like guardians flanking him on both sides. He was continuously in awe of the sights and sounds of his paradise home and of his new life after death. As he casually strolled along, he was suddenly confronted by the sight of a giant Bengal tiger with vibrant golden eyes slowly passing from one side of the immense hallway to the other. The magnificent beast barely glanced in his direction to see who might be approaching as he travelled towards the lush, green landscape that was now his domain. No need to worry about hunters or predators here. The large pads of his giant feet barely made a sound as he quietly moved on slowly. The tip of his long tail was the last thing Levi saw as the magnificent creature disappeared into the multicolored wild flowers that engulfed him.

Levi was calm. If this had been an encounter on Earth with this animal, he knew he would soon be dead. But because he was already technically dead, there was nothing to worry about. There was no man-eating going on here—just peace and harmony. He had yet to actually touch a lion or bear or any other carnivore since he had arrived, but it was something he planned to do eventually. The animals and birds were amazing. As an Earthling, his only real interactions with animals had been the family pets. He was now surrounded by every type of species known to man, most of which he knew nothing about. The access to information was also endless. He could spend infinite time simply discovering new and unique creatures and flora. Oh, there was so much to do and to learn here. Levi would pace himself as usual; he had plenty of time to experience and learn as much as he wanted. It was an amazing feeling.

The expansive view of Plane 5 from this vantage point was breathtaking. Levi, like all who passed over, had had no idea what to expect when he arrived, other than what he had read in books or seen in movies about the afterlife. There were so many versions, concepts, and speculations about this place. It was truly mind-boggling. But Levi was now convinced that there were no descriptions anywhere that could ever compare to the reality of actually being here, and he was sure that was the way it was meant to be. Indescribable.

*You really just have to see it for yourself,* he thought to himself as he stopped to gaze at the panorama of the fantastic world before him. He would never be tired of taking in this view, which was a good thing, considering that this was where he would spend eternity, something that was quickly accepted by all upon arrival on Plane 3 and any other Plane they might visit on the other side. As he made his way toward his destination at the end of the hall, he thought about his life on Earth and what his family would think if they could see him now. Completely healthy, happy, and strong. Nothing like he was when he left them, and even though he had been here for a while, everything was still a wonder.

He, like his fellow souls, found comfort in knowing that someday they would all be with their family and friends in this wonderful place.

Levi quickly stopped in front of two large wooden doors that must have been at least twenty feet tall, with finely sculpted golden handles. The doors were breathtaking and were carved with the precision of a superior craftsman. Maybe one of the Renaissance artists themselves? He would have to study up on his art history. He knew that the intricate designs in front of him had powerful meaning. Everything you could see and touch on Plane 5 had meaning. It was all about learning and evolving. One day, he would stay and study these amazing images and embrace their beauty with full knowledge and appreciation.

As he stood before the massive doors, he felt small not only in stature but also in the overall scheme of things. He was not a tall man at 5'7", and these doors reminded him of that fact. They were just doors—not a comment on his height or anything else—he told himself. Doors. No walls, but lots of really large doors. It was a thing here. The afterlife was an open and welcoming place, but it seemed you were always entering a door of some kind leading to something important. It was clear messaging determined by some supreme advertising agency, he imagined. There had to be plenty of talented souls here and no end to what they would be able to create with unlimited resources. A dream job of sorts.

He remembered how he had felt when he first arrived on Plane 3 and saw the large gates that awaited him. No, they were not pearly—just big and beautifully adorned with cherubs and all kinds of symbols he didn't recognize or understand. With his mother Helene at his side, he had been somewhat overwhelmed and curious at the same time. He felt safe and beyond happy to see his mother. They held hands as he was warmly welcomed by friends and animals that he had long ago lost. Unbelievable feelings of love had filled his heart. Levi knew that he was home. Forever at peace.

Even soon after his arrival, there were practically no explanations necessary. Things just made sense. It was always pleasant and inviting. There were guides to assist you and explain  anything you couldn't grasp. If you had an inquiry, it seemed that there was always someone nearby to help you with your thoughts and dilemmas. No stress or illness here. Everyone was healthy and happy. Like himself, lots of people had endured grave illnesses on Earth and were finally free of pain and suffering. It was odd at first to be around all healthy people. He had gotten used to the hardships of living an Earthly life. It seemed like everyone on Earth had some kind of issue, and there was plenty of emotional and physical discomfort to go around there. That was definitely one of the best things about being dead. No pain.

There were plenty of new doors opening for you here, leading to something wonderful and unexpected. Levi was getting used to the doors.

However, he was a bit nervous now as he craned his neck upward at these doors. He knew that at the end of the final course on Plane 5, it was required for pre-Elite trainees to become an Assistant during several Class X Human Recoveries. His ultimate goal was to become a Plane 6 Elite. He had thought long and hard about it, and he had worked diligently and tirelessly just to attain Assistant status.

Assistant. It didn't sound very important, but he knew that to get the real job he wanted, he would have to prove himself like all the others before him, and he was more than willing to do whatever was asked of him. The time was now. Was he ready now? There was so much he did not know about the Elites themselves. There was a general understanding that they were private and mysterious. Not easy to get to know or understand. Although at one time they were human, they now dealt with humans from a whole new perspective. It was complicated for sure, especially when there were demons and evil entities involved. Levi knew this was going to be a wild ride and a potentially dangerous one at that.

Of course, dangerous also had new meaning now. Being dead kind of took the scariness out of actually dying some horrible death or dealing with injuries and pain. But there was the possibility of losing your life again on Earth, which meant not being able to complete the training to become an Elite being. He knew that that dream would then be over. There was a strict rule about not completing missions and dying again. Seemed a bit unfair to Levi. You were already dead, so what was the big deal?

But like everything else here, it was all so defined and purposeful. Losing the ability to become a Plane 6 Elite being was hard to think about, and just being in this wonderful place was not such a bad thing. Levi would let the chips fall where they may. Either way would be highly satisfying.

There were wild stories about Class X Recoveries, and it seemed that they rarely went as planned. He would be working with an Elite being from Plane 6 who had a reputation for being a little bit of a cowboy, an Elite who did things outside the box. It was all pretty mysterious and not typical of Earth scenarios at all. Things were done a bit differently here, for sure. He was excited and a bit apprehensive all at the same time just thinking about becoming a Plane 6 Elite himself one day. He would have skills and powers unlike other human souls while experiencing great adventures and seeing places and things unavailable to him while on Earth.

He could have studied to do basic human recoveries or animal recoveries. He loved animals. Still, he wanted the chance to work with and eventually become a higher being, a super being, and that meant Class X Recoveries. There were even stories about Plane 6 Elites going totally rogue. Levi was not sure what that meant because The Creator had a hand in everything, and it seemed unlikely that they could actually get away with anything. All of this would be explained when Levi became more deeply involved and had finished his first assignment.

Class X humans were different from other people who lived on Earth in that they were extremely powerful and had strong and unrealistic ties to the Earthly plane. It was never easy for them to make the transition to Plane 2. Levi thought to himself that if they only knew how wonderful and peaceful it could be, they would not make the process so difficult. That was naive thinking, and he knew it. Crossing over was unique to every human and animal, and they would never know what it was like on the other side until they made the transition.

While he was deep in thought, and without a touch of his hand, the giant doors slowly began to open, and Levi cautiously stepped into the enormous space. There were thirty-foot ceilings above him, more white marble pillars, and a giant alabaster desk straight ahead in the middle of the room. It was all so stunning and marvelous. While there were no angels with harps playing and singing, it would have been a perfect fit. There was nothing like this on Earth or any other planet. The ceilings were painted with frescos, like the beautiful churches and structures on Earth in Italy and around the world, only bigger. And more realistic, if that's possible. The perfectly detailed images looked as though they could depart the paintings at any time, gently float down to the floor, and join the conversation. He wanted to stand and just take it all in, but this was an extremely important meeting. He would need to stay focused.

Two people were sitting behind the intricately sculptured desk. There were no drawers or pencils laying around. It was pristine and shiny, with nothing but a slim screen that was built into the top of the flat surface and elevated slightly for the two people to easily view. He half expected to see an Apple logo on the back. There was no logo, and the use of such machines or technology was simply a preference in the afterlife. They were simply a way to make new and learning human souls feel comfortable. There were no such devices on Plane 6.

Levi could not see what was on the screen, but he knew that it was some kind of visual reference system. In the hereafter, the mind is the vault, and communication is either telepathic or verbal, whatever you prefer. Levi had heard that higher-level souls pretty much only did the telepathic thing. It was all pretty cool and sometimes intimidating. Keeping one's thoughts to one's self could be challenging. There were techniques just for that purpose. Kind of like cell phones on Earth, you could block telepathy from happening on the other side from another soul if you chose to, and you generally had to be eye-to-eye for it to be effective when you did want to communicate. Levi was pretty good at it. But once you became a Plane 6 Elite, all bets were off. They could delve into the minds of whomever they wanted and whenever they wanted, for the most part. It was all fascinating, and he was eager to learn all about it.

There were two beautifully patterned overstuffed chairs in front of the desk for guests to sit and talk. Again, not really necessary, as one did not get tired in this environment. It was simply a way to create a familiar experience, and it added comfort and continuity for souls who preferred the Earth home environment. Most Earth humans had never seen a real fresco, let alone been surrounded by the likes of these spectacular masterpieces. Levi was feeling lucky to be in the grand space, as the man before him stood.

Cyrus was tall and handsome and dressed in a gold and white robe. He welcomed Levi and asked him to sit and relax. Levi was happy to sit but was not sure he could relax. It was all pretty intimidating. An elegant woman next to the man was dressed in a gold and soft-rose colored dress.

In a kind tone, she said, "Oh, Levi, we are so happy to finally be at this juncture with you in your training." She smiled sweetly. "You have worked so hard, and we are always thrilled when our proteges finally arrive at the place where they can be of so much help to us."

The woman who stood before him was stunningly beautiful. Although her hair was pure white, she did not look a day over 30. And even though they were called The Ancients, it was obvious that they were advanced in intelligence but not in physical appearance. Again, a preference. You could decide at which age you preferred to be viewed. Levi had picked 40 for himself. He liked that age. And had he not been sick when he died, he would have liked the way he looked and felt about himself then, too. Although he would have preferred to be a little taller in Earth life, he felt the need in death to maintain his shorter stature as a way of learning and adjusting to his issues about being short. He wanted to get past all of that and just feel good about himself. That was all up to him. It was easy in the afterlife to come to terms with shortcomings, as there was no judgement about such things. You were accepted as is. And of course, most souls in the afterlife had chosen to look their very best.

After a few minutes in the soft and comfortable chair, Levi was beginning to feel a little better. More calm. He had heard that The Ancients had that effect on people, and they definitely made the process effortless. Levi had passed all of his training courses on Plane 5 with flying colors and felt that he could handle any job that was put before him. He would be an Assistant to a Plane 6 Elite. Even though time was different on the other side, there still was a kind of time and order to things. There was some waiting for things, even though it never really felt like it did on Earth. Probably because you always knew that it wasn't ever going to be bad. Nothing to worry about here. Just plenty to look forward to and some nerves about moments like these, but only when something big was expected of you. It was completely your choice. Levi knew that he could live an afterlife full of adventures that were not dangerous and spend nothing but time enjoying the numerous opportunities to learn and grow, which was something that was encouraged at all times if possible. Not to mention the moments with his son, his mom, friends, and animals that he had loved on Earth—and some people he had not loved so much on Earth. Amends were made, and they now added to the fullness of this circle of soul friends on Plane 3.

The Ancients were now conversing and looking at their screen, while Levi thought about the Elites. There was heavy speculation about these beings, and they did not spend time on Plane 5 unless absolutely necessary or to visit family and friends. It was possible to interact with them but only on special occasions and for meetings such as this. Assistants were not allowed to mingle with the Elite with whom they would be working with prior to an assignment, so he was not at all sure who that would be. That was the deal, and he wondered if he had ever seen the Elite he would partner with, at some point while he was in training on Plane 5. He would soon find out.

Levi had heard a lot of peculiar things about them in general. They had lived on Earth, transitioned to the afterlife, and through hard work with special practice sessions and exclusive interactions and gifts from the Creator, had achieved amazing super powers and abilities. Although a bit apprehensive, Levi was fascinated by the prospect of actually getting to work side-by-side with one. In the afterlife, everyone is not privy to all information all the time, despite what may be said on the internet. There are rules and unique strategies created for each human, animal, and creature that passes over. Everyone eventually has a job or purpose. Even though it did not feel like work, it was meaningful and important for the balance of the Universe, and the Universe was on a very tight timeline. Not a lot of room for error or Earthly humans trying to change their destined death dates; hence the Class X Recoveries.

The Ancients looked up from their screens and engaged with Levi. They chatted about his successful education and promising career. It really was all quite relaxed now. He could do this. No problem.

There was a sudden change in the air…in the breeze. Something was about to happen; he could feel it.

# Chapter Two

As Dani briskly walked down the hallway, her long, waist-length, auburn ponytail swayed back and forth in an almost rhythmic motion, sweeping across her jade-green bodysuit. She was tall and sleek like a cat, and her perfectly fit figure was out of this world. In her stealth-like fashion, she glided across the black stone walkway with confidence, eager to speak with The Ancients about her new assignment.

This, of course, was not her first Class X Human Recovery. She knew the drill and just needed to be updated about some of the final details. There would be a new Assistant, Levi, whom she would have to meet. She had studied him from afar, as was part of her planning phase. She always felt that she could handle these assignments herself, but it was mandatory that all Plane 6 Elites be involved in the advancement of an Assistant's journey to become a Plane 6 Elite themselves. And because the Elites were so mentally and physically superior to other souls, they needed help sometimes "fitting back in" to the Earth plane scenario. The Assistants were there to help them with that and to provide other Earthly services as needed.

Upon entering the Earth plane, Assistants became human-like and were visible to humans and all other Earth species. Dani, on the other hand, had un-Earthlike skills and various physical forms available to her, so her semi-human Assistant would definitely come in handy to cover for her when necessary. Her ability to become invisible at will could create all kinds of interesting challenges for her Assistants. While they would be looking out for each other most of the time, it was expected that at this level, they could handle their jobs independently. Elites could be aloof and tricky to understand some of the time. It was common knowledge that communication between Elites and Assistants was a learned skill. Part of the on-the-job training.

Approaching the outer doors to the Palace, Dani did not miss a step, and the big doors swung open as if she had willed them to do so. She had received her dossier on the subject of her transition and was ready to get the process started. As she entered the large room, all conversation abruptly ceased. Everything stopped. Even the breeze seemed to stop blowing. It was clear that a highly powerful being had entered the room, and even The Ancients were clearly taken aback by her imposing presence. She approached the desk and firmly planted her feet directly in front of the two people now focused on and staring directly at her. She had been here many times before, and they had dealt with her unique quirks many times as well. Dani was legendary among the Elite crowd, not only for her commanding presence but also for her ability to get any job done with relative ease regardless of how many evil entities and demons were involved. One would think that on the other side, these Elite beings would be the stuff of Earthly heroes and characters you might see in a blockbuster movie. But it was actually quite the opposite. Souls who were heroes and law enforcement types on Earth tended to be mellow beings dedicated to an afterlife of peace and quiet reflection, while those who led relatively peace-loving or fairly ordinary lives on Earth hungered for the action and fulfillment of their superhero dreams. Dani fit that profile and was now one of the most powerful of her kind.

Levi was mesmerized by the stunning creature who stood next to him. He didn't move and felt incredibly meek and small in the big chair. He was a little embarrassed by his bashful demeanor and was completely speechless. As it turned out, there would be very little speaking from that moment on, at least by the Plane 6 Elite. They used telepathic communication for the most part and were annoyed when they had to actually speak verbally. So old-school. Levi was aware of this and proceeded to sit and stare at her as The Ancients began to speak —verbally—which Levi assumed was for his benefit. He was well-trained in telepathy, of course. Everyone was doing it. It was the preferred means of communication in the afterlife, but he still enjoyed using the verbal communication technique used by many of the Plane 5 trainees. He secretly hoped that the Elite would not hold this against him. Not a good foot to start off on.

"Dani, darling, so good to see you!" Sasha said with great enthusiasm.

Cyrus was beaming as well, as though he was proudly looking at his own daughter. While they were seemingly genuine in their enthusiasm, Levi could not help but sense a bit of what he could only describe as fear emanating from them both. As he looked at Dani, he wondered why. She was stunningly beautiful, feminine, and seemed pleasant enough, even though she had not even acknowledged that he was in the room. That was odd, since he was going to be spending significant Earth time with her, and she would depend on him. Right?

As soon as he had that thought, Dani turned and looked directly at him. Not with a smile—just a piercing look that he felt to the core of his soul. Her green eyes were the most beautiful eyes he had ever seen. He almost didn't mind that he was petrified, possibly shaking a bit. He hoped that she wouldn't notice.

But of course, Dani noticed everything. One of her dynamic attributes, no doubt. The message was loud and clear. Speak when spoken to and think when needed. Could he actually do that? Probably not. This relationship was definitely going to be a challenge.

Dani turned back to The Ancients. She was all business. No need for introductions or pleasantries. "When will I and the Zengats be leaving and from which specified location?" she asked with a somber look.

The Ancients flashed each other a look and were quick to give her the information that she requested via a chip. She reached out her perfect hand with her perfectly painted green nails and grabbed the drive. She paused for a moment and did some kind of mind-meld with them.

This was all new to Levi. Even though he knew it would happen, he had never seen it happen. It was intense. He could actually see some kind of aura emanating from the three souls, pulsing back and forth. Dani was taking it all in. This particular set of information was for the Elite only. Levi had his marching orders. This was secret stuff. No doubt having to do with demons and the like. Levi was trying to follow along, but his telepathic capabilities couldn't and weren't supposed to penetrate this kind of action. He quickly remembered that he did not need to understand this part anyway. What he needed to know was on his pad, and in his head, to be accessed as needed. Details would get worked out once they hit the Earth plane. *Even having the basic Assistant knowledge was a powerful feeling*, he thought to himself. But he was now understanding what real power felt like on the other side, and it was standing next to him.

When reentering the Earth plane, past soul senses and abilities were somewhat dulled due to the atmospheric changes and plane-level contrast, so it was good to have references available at all times. He could not afford to be off his game at any point during this process. Elites, of course, were not affected by the limitations of being on Earth. They had mastered the ability to basically maintain their afterlife skills and thinking without any problems related to the atmosphere or anything else, which were all things that Levi was looking forward to possessing someday. She had mentioned Zengats. As the mind-melding was coming to a close, Levi was wondering what or who that meant. This was also new. He had never heard of the Zengats. Right then, Dani reached out behind her like a mom beckoning a small child to come and hold their hand.

At that moment, a huge, hairy, black, wolf-like creature entered the room. It was the size of a large male lion, and it moved slowly toward Dani's left side between her and his chair and sat. Levi noticed that it wasn't wearing any sort of a collar and appeared to be free to roam and do as it pleased, like all of the other species in the afterlife. It looked over at Levi as he sat frozen with dread. The animal blinked its ruby-red eyes at Levi as a small bit of saliva dripped from one of its long fangs, as if to say, "I am a Zengat, you idiot." The beast's large eyes then turned to a caramel brown color, and it fixed its gaze on The Ancients, who were by then sweating profusely and fanning themselves.

Levi was trying hard not to think of anything, but it was inevitable. *She said Zengats…was that plural? As if one wasn't enough.*

Dani chose to ignore his thought. She looked at Levi with somewhat softened eyes and telepathically said, "See you at Crystaline Circle, Levi." She proceeded to leave the room with her Zengat close behind. The room suddenly lightened up, and even the soft breeze seemed willing to return.

The Ancients were now sitting quietly behind the desk looking at Levi with sympathetic gazes.

Levi smiled nervously and said, "Well, she sure is somethin'! And that Zengat…wow…really, really big, and black, and—big."

Cyrus spoke in a level tone. "Dani is one of the most extraordinary Plane 6 souls to ever exist. You have been given a great opportunity to learn from the best, Levi. She can be a little hard around the edges at first, but make no mistake, she always gets the job done. And beneath that somewhat rigid exterior beats a heart of gold, as they say. You may never witness that, but it is there. You must remember a few things, Levi. The Zengats will protect her to the death. They are ethereal beings that cannot be destroyed by any Earthly means. They are used for purposes of protection and intimidation at times if needed during complicated transitions. They can be quite friendly, if they take a liking to you."

With a careful smile, Sasha added, "Best if you just let them be."

Levi managed a semi-confident nod.

"Also, Dani is in charge at all times. She knows what to do. You are there for Earthly support. Keep her on task. Help her to blend in. Your training has taught you well. These recoveries can take several Earth days. I am sure you will get along just fine," Cyrus said with a wink.

Somehow the thought of trying to help Dani do anything seemed completely ridiculous. Not remotely doable. And making friends with giant beasts from hell was not on Levi's list of interesting or safe things to do. Where did they come from? He had never seen anything like them roaming around on Plane 3, 4 or 5. They must only live on Plane 6. Maybe they were strays from Plane 1. He would have to look into that.

Levi was given a final set of instructions via his chip from The Ancients, which he inserted into a pad that he kept with him at all times. It was a nice option when there was a lot of information that needed to be retained and accessed. Most people who were not on assignment in the afterlife did not carry or need pads. The pads were mostly for transition teams and higher learning experiences.

With that, The Ancients bowed and wished Levi the best of luck and thanked him profusely for partaking in such an important mission. Was it his imagination, or did they seem very relieved and anxious to get out of there?

As Levi was leaving the great room and entering the long hallway, he realized that he had not felt any fear at all when he saw the giant animals wandering the grounds—the lions, tigers, bears, and the like. They all seemed so tame and not the least bit intimidating. And not at all Zengat-like. The Zengats were something else. Completely different. Dangerous. Levi knew he was going to have to bring his A-game to this adventure. He said a little prayer.

# Chapter Three

As Dani left the palace, she was reminded of her arrival on Plane 3. It was all so far behind her now, but because time was so different on the other side, the memories came flooding back quickly, which was frowned upon in cases where they were disturbing or uncomfortable for crossed-over souls to think about. But as an Elite, she could access whatever thoughts and memories she wanted whenever she wanted. One would think that it was a perk of being an Elite. It was actually one of the downsides, if there were any. Most transitioned human souls were quite content to move on and past any bad memories from Earth and get on with their interesting and adventure-filled time on the other side. Travel, meeting all kinds of amazing and interesting souls, and higher learning opportunities were always available and encouraged. Not to mention physical endeavors and social events with the ability to participate in ways that they never would have thought possible when they were on Earth.

Dani had evolved beyond her wildest imagination, and she was proud to be a Plane 6 Elite. It was not an easy road, indeed and not one that a lot of people wanted to pursue. Most humans transitioning from Earth simply wanted to be in a beautiful and peaceful place at last. They were thrilled to reunite with loved ones and animals that they had left behind when they died. While Dani missed her family, her fiancé, and friends, she wanted to achieve a higher level of responsibility and to be of help to her fellow souls. She wanted to make a difference in the world, even if it was from the other side.

Elite status was only available to the few souls who could master the training and who were willing to deal with some highly unsavory characters and extremely challenging situations. Dani had worked hard, and she felt that she was ready and able to master any needed traits and abilities she would need to accomplish her tasks on her Earth plane assignments. She was a master at her craft, and it was understood that she was the one to fear on the Earth plane—not some silly demons or evil entities. Of course, the demons and evil entities would never really understand what they were up against with an Elite. It would play out as planned for the most part, and the demons would get their due.

There were stories about Elites gone rogue. Dani was aware of this, and she knew that at some point, that might be another kind of recovery that she would have to partake in. For now, it was all about this assignment. The Earth had changed since she died, and there were plenty of evil people and situations that she would have to confront and deal with whenever she performed a crossover. Normal human transitions from Earth to Plane 3 were handled by experienced Plane 5 souls. They were quite capable of handling the typical death scenarios, and there were rarely complications. If something wasn't going well, Plane 6 Elites could step in and help with the crossover. Animal transitions were completed by trained Plane 4 souls and rarely required any assistance. There might be the occasional human involved, which complicated things, but generally speaking, animal deaths were the easiest to manage. It was always heartening to see their arrivals and how joyous they were to see their long-lost families and friends. Wild animals and other species were reunited with their herds and the groups they spent time with on Earth.

Plane 6 Elites basically never helped with any souls on the lower planes unless absolutely necessary. They were specifically trained for special and difficult circumstances. Their powers were extraordinary and unique. Only The Ancients and the Creator were fully aware of their capabilities. At least this was what they thought. There were rumors that the Plane 6 Elites had powers that even the highest orders were not privy to. It went without saying, literally, that they were pretty off-the-charts, and containing them was part of the challenge for their superiors. While they could always get their assignments done, they sometimes went off-script, and it was always a hope that they would not do anything to change the Universal time algorithms. They were given some leeway and free will, but it was understood that they should stick to the protocols outlined during their training at all times.

Assistants would never really know what all of those powers entailed. It was actually better that way. Assistants were meant to fit in on the Earth plane. Blend in, so to speak. Do as they were told. Try not to get killed…or die again. Dani was a super being now, and blending in was not her strong suit. Her appearance alone would draw attention. It was all her choice. She did not care what people thought. Any reaction that she saw that was out of the ordinary would soon be forgotten with a blink of her eye. Literally. She could get away with murder in a public place if she wanted to.

On the Earth plane, her power was unmatched, but Plane 6 Elites could be confronted with some nasty demons conjured by Earth humans, which could threaten the lives of the souls that they were targeting. The Elites were called in to make those transitions, and they were the only beings who could take temporary human form at times when they were dealing with their Earthly tasks, sometimes making them vulnerable to Earthly death. Those were rare cases, and it was generally known that they were invincible and had adequate protection. There had been a few cases of this happening, and it was sad to see an Elite die again and lose the powers that allowed them to continue on in their super power position. But it was all part of the Universal plan. Dani had no intentions of finding herself in that situation. She would rely on her Assistant, if needed, and her large furry friends and would complete her business on Earth successfully.

Plane 6 Elites did not carry traditional weapons. Their powers were their weapons, and of course, their Zengats. Dani was always careful and smart. Her instincts were amazing, and she was able to keep her emotions in check. Most of the time.

As an Elite, she, like all others who passed over, was supposed to keep the past behind her as much as possible and to stay focused on the tasks at hand and the future, but Dani would never forget the devastating events that had led to her death on Earth or the evil men who were responsible. She knew it was going to play a part in her next assignment. Somehow, some way.

Dani had enjoyed her time on Earth as a young girl and grew up in a beautiful, small town in the Northeast region of the US. She was raised on a farm, and her greatest loves were the animals. Her parents, John and Nancy, had raised her to be kind and caring. While she excelled in school and did the usual kid things with her friends, she focused a lot of her time on her Friesian horse, Cole, who was her best friend.

Big, black, and powerful, Cole was amazing, and they would spend hours riding the trails in the rural hills just happy to be together. He had been a gift from her doting father after her mother died. Together, they ran the big farm, which included several other horses, goats, and pet chickens. Her mother had died from cancer when Dani was 17 years old, and her dad had picked up the pieces and wanted desperately to make all of Dani's dreams come true. One of those dreams was to have a black horse. She didn't care what breed or gender, it just had to be black.

He'd guessed it was for the love of the horse in the book *Black Beauty* that she had seemed to read over and over when she was younger. So he searched until he came upon a breeder of black horses, which he was surprised was not far from their ranch. He made a phone call, jumped into his truck that very day, and as soon as he walked into Frank Kenning's barn, he knew he would find Dani's horse.

Frank had a stable of champion Friesians, a breed that Dani's father knew nothing about. The horses on his farm had always been rescue animals, and he was happy to save them no matter what breed they were. They were a mix of Quarter Horses, Arabians, and Grade stock. Frank was happy to explain the Friesian breed to John, and within a brief amount of time, Dani's father was sold on getting one of his beautiful animals for his daughter. This would be a purebred breed with a champion bloodline. John was exhilarated at the thought. He knew his daughter would have been happy with any black horse, but this just seemed to be the right fit right now.

Once they discussed price, which was way beyond anything that John could pay, Frank quickly whisked him away to a horse at the very end of the barn. John knew this was never going to happen. He didn't have that kind of money. But he wanted to meet this horse. And he was stunning. His name was

Cole, and John knew that Dani would be thrilled. Still, the cost of this animal was putting him out of reach. John told Frank that while this would be the most amazing animal that he could give to his girl, he simply could not afford it. He told Frank that Dani was getting her real estate license and that maybe someday they could afford a horse like this after she sold a few houses. He also told Frank that all of his animals were rescued and that it wasn't a priority to have this spectacular horse in their barn, as badly as he wanted it for her.

Frank listened, recognizing the heartfelt sincerity in the man who stood before him. In a moment of highly unusual generosity, Frank agreed to let him take the horse and give him a wonderful home. John was stunned. He thought that there must be something wrong with the horse. Frank assured him that the sire was his grand champion, Black Magic's Folly, and that Cole was one of the finest in his barn. He wanted him to have a loving home. Frank knew that John's daughter would be the perfect person for him. He didn't need the money, and it felt good to do something charitable. Cole didn't need rescuing, and he would be among other horses and adored by a young girl. Perfect. He said he would get the paperwork together for John and deliver the horse in the morning.

It was all too much for John to believe. How was this possible? Frank was going to give him a $50,000 horse. John, of course, did not know who he was dealing with. He did know that Frank was very wealthy, sure, but the guy didn't even know John or Dani or even where the horse would live. It was all so strange. What John didn't know was that no one even entered Frank's property that was not thoroughly vetted along with their entire family. Frank knew that Dani's mother had recently died and that Dani was beginning a career in real estate. She was doing well and was an expert rider. He trusted her with his horse, and he might be able to persuade her to work for him one day soon. Frank could hire whomever he wanted, but what he wanted these days were honest and smart people to increase the level of quality of his semi-legitimate business. Real estate.

So it was done. John had just made the deal of a lifetime. This horse would be the dream come true that he wanted for his daughter.

He rushed home and told Dani that he had a very special delivery coming for her in the morning. He could hardly contain himself. She couldn't imagine what he was talking about. Flowers? It wasn't her birthday. What could it be?

Dani had finished her chores the following morning, and she saw her father come running to find her.

He was excited, and he blurted out, "He's here!"

*Who's here?* Dani thought.

Before she could get an answer, she saw a truck and horse trailer coming down the driveway. She had never seen that truck before, but she suddenly got a feeling that something big was about to happen.

The logo on the side of the truck was familiar to Dani. She knew all about Frank Kenning's Friesians. She had never met him but had secretly dreamed of one day just going to his ranch to see his beautiful horses. The man got out of the truck, walked around, and opened the trailer gate.

Dani's dad looked at her and said, "He is for you. All yours! And his name is Cole."

As he came off the trailer, she could only cry with joy. How was this possible? This horse had to cost a small fortune. A fortune that she knew her father did not have. She blocked that out of her mind. He was magnificent. And he was hers! He was indeed black as coal and so beautiful that she couldn't believe that he belonged to her. Frank Kenning stepped forward and introduced himself. Dani was a bit intimidated but so thankful that she impulsively hugged him. Frank smiled and told her that if she ever needed anything or any help with Cole, to call him. It was all so unreal. As Frank pulled out of the driveway, Dani had a feeling that she would be seeing him again. And it wouldn't be about horses.

Life on the ranch was hard at times but full of adventures. She already loved Cole and was forever grateful to the two men who had made it possible. Her dad and Frank Kenning. She had no idea where this horse and life would take her. All she knew was that she had just met the love of her life, and for the first time since she lost her mom, she was truly happy again.

She had many wonderful years with her beloved horse, but when Dani turned 21, Cole became ill, and for months, Dani and her family tried desperately to save him. His illness was a mystery, and she felt so helpless. Frank spared no expense trying to remedy the problem, but the beautiful horse eventually died, which broke Dani's heart.

This memory was forever burned into her mind. It was only when she herself died that she was reunited with her beloved horse and mother. It was an amazing reunion. Like time had stopped and they were all together again, only this time, it would be forever. It was important that humans on Earth were not sure whether they would see their loved ones or animal friends again. The knowing could cause all kinds of problems for the Creator's plans. So, the heartache of loss would continue for all living humans until they would all meet again someday, and Dani had felt every bit of that heartache.

On Plane 6, Dani spent her time with Cole and all her pets from her Earth life, along with lots of homeless and wild animals that she had encountered as well. Only Plane 6 Elites could enter and live on Plane 6. It was highly complicated there. There were sophisticated training sessions, and regular meetings and updates about potential and upcoming Class X Human Transitions were always somewhere on the schedule.

Because animals were allowed at the request of an Elite, it was never lonely there. They kept her company, and she was content to be an Elite and doing Elite things. She could travel to see her mother and other family and friends on Plane 3 whenever she wanted, but most of the time, her focus was her ongoing training and evolution on Plane 6. It was as she wanted it. All was good on the other side.

# Chapter Four

The Zengats were not of Earth origin and did not roam freely on Plane 6. They were creatures conceived by the Creator to assist in the transitions of special subjects only. Did they have souls? Did they have compassion? No one knew for sure. Dani was assigned five Zengats to be at her disposal as she deemed necessary. Although they did not come with names, Dani named them and always pretended that they were really dogs, even though they were clearly not. They possessed great powers that they used to intimidate and to protect. They acquired some traits of normal dogs with time spent on Earth, but there was no mistaking that they were killing machines wrapped in scary wolves' clothing.

The Zengats were the only beings from the other side that were allowed to kill a human on Earth if absolutely necessary. The Universal time algorithms would be adjusted for those particular occasions. Again, Dani didn't really want protection, as her powers would serve her well, but because Elite beings sometimes became vulnerable when they entered the Earth plane, the Zengats were needed. If she died an Earthly death, Dani would lose her Elite status and would never be able to obtain it again. She would transition to Plane 3, where she would live out eternity. Because the chances of that happening were so rare, it almost seemed senseless to have the Zengats at all; however, for the purposes of getting humans' attention in short order, they were well worth it. The same fate existed for the Assistants, as they too could die again by Earthly means. Because their job was to work with Elite Plane 6 beings, they were often exposed to dangerous and life-threatening situations. The Zengats would come in very handy indeed.

There were thousands of normal transitions occurring every day on the Earth plane with the assistance of Planes 4 and 5 trained souls. It was always possible that Dani could cross the path of one of these beings during her assignments, including this one, but these missions were never social visits, and the communication with other Plane-level beings would be minimal at best. Preferably there would be none at all. The Planes 4 and 5 beings could only be seen by the person they were transitioning at the time of their death, Dani, Levi, and the

Zengats, and they were strictly directed to keep clear of Plane 6 Elites unless absolutely necessary.

On the Earth plane, Dani had had a young man in her life at the time of her death. His name was Adam. He was her perfect match. They met in the small town they both lived near and were immediately taken with each other. Their mutual love for horses drew them even closer together. He spent hours at her farm, and they rode horses and enjoyed life together. Both of their careers were just taking off, and the world was their oyster. He was an equine veterinarian, and she was a realtor. They had gotten engaged sitting on the backs of their horses, Cole and Scout, and looked forward to a wonderful life together filled with love, animals, and lots of green pastures to run free whenever they wanted. Perhaps the death of Cole was some foreboding sign of what was to come. They had mourned together, and it had put a dark cloud over the planning of their wedding. Still, they stood firm with their plans because they wanted to be together so badly.

It was not meant to be. When Dani died, Adam was beyond devastated at her passing and struggled to move on. His whole world seemed to become dark, and the sadness was numbing. He had grown up in a broken home and had lived with his mom until she died right before he met Dani, who was the spark that he had needed to move on and finally find happiness. He had so looked forward to their future and the life they would build together filled with animals and hopefully children. Two, to be exact. They had it all planned. Dani's father would eventually sell the farm, and together they would find their own dream ranch and create a fantastic life. And they had done exactly that. Their new property was under contract, and John had an offer on the farm. They were going to build a guest house on the property, where John would live out his days amongst his beloved animals, his daughter, and her husband and new family.

Best laid plans, as they say.

Adam would never forget his beloved girl, and it would leave a hole in his heart for the rest of his life.

Against the basic rules of the afterlife, Dani thought of him often and was now going to be in the general vicinity of where he would be on Earth. Dani knew that The Ancients had to have been aware of this fact before they gave her this assignment. Perhaps this was some kind of test. It would be a difficult process, she knew, but she was secretly looking forward to seeing him again, even if it was only from a distance.

Prior to a Class X Human Recovery, Elites are given huge amounts of information on their subject, which they then file away in their mind for later use. Dani was curious about Adam but did not want to draw any attention to her interest. There is a database of transitions available to all Elite 6 beings that contains basic information about all souls' transitions and life status on Earth. She checked on a regular basis. Adam was still alive and living in the same small town where they had fallen in love. The same small town she would now be visiting.

It had been 10 Earth years since her death. It would be against the rules to seek him out at any time during one of her transitions. Not to mention the fact that it would be a bit of a shock for him if she suddenly showed up. While on the Earth plane, she would take her past human form with some small enhancements, such as hair color and super powers. She would look normal to people who saw her. Well, sort of normal. And then there would be her Assistant tagging along. The two of them could not be more different. *The odd couple, for sure*, she thought. Again, she didn't care. She had a job to do, and odd couple or not, she would succeed.

The thought of seeing her beloved Adam was a curse and a blessing. She would look the same as she did 10 years ago. He would of course be ten years older. The thought of seeing him was exhilarating to her. Even though she knew she would be reunited with him eventually, she couldn't help wanting to see him now. In his Earthly form. Like it was before she left. Would he be in love with someone new? This was the downside of looking into past relationships after you passed over. People moved on. Whether you liked it or not. She purposely never looked to find that information about him, preferring to think that he was the same, things were the same. Some people who suffered loss stay mired in misery and pain, but most moved on to new people and experiences. She selfishly hoped that he wasn't totally miserable but that he was still single and thinking about her. She would soon find out.

At the time of transition from Earth to Plane 3, memory was selectively eliminated. When the person was deemed ready, more information was revealed about their final days, especially in the case of violent or traumatic deaths. This was all in the best interest of the person's well-being and ability to move forward and be at peace with their time on Earth.

Dani had gone through the basic crossover indoctrination just like every other human, and she was sure that she was over the past and ready to move on. She might have done that eventually if she had not been given this particular assignment. The Ancients knew that they needed a powerful Elite to deal with this situation, and they had to know that it would cause conflict with her.

Dani did not know that The Ancients believed that if she was able to accomplish this transition, she could be elevated to the position of Supreme Guide, a goal that Dani was hoping one day to achieve. It was basically a teaching position with very little physical Earth plane interaction. She would be a guide and instructor for Elites and a consultant for The Ancients. She would also have full range of powers and the ability to interact with the Creator at will, something only allowed for Supreme Guides. The Creator was, in a few words, Master of the Universe. There were several planes above Plane 6 that were allocated to angels and guides, and they were a busy bunch. Dani was not interested in becoming an angel; there was not enough excitement and challenge for her. It was a wonderful thing, but it also had its limitations.

You would have to give up all connections and communications with your Earthly family, friends, and animals. You would only be in service to the Creator and the humans that were worthy of your help and guidance, which fortunately included most of them. The advantage of having no ties to anyone was the ability to be of targeted service and help without distraction. But it just wasn't a good fit for Dani. She liked the action and challenges that came with a more complicated existence.

She looked forward to the challenges of working with Elite wannabes and showing them the ropes and a few tricks that she had learned along her many and varied paths, some even the Creator was unaware of. Another perk of being Dani. She was trusted and had proven herself time and time again. She knew the weaknesses of being human, and it was no different being a super soul. There were weaknesses. The Creator and The Ancients knew this and allowed free will. It was all about learning and becoming enlightened at the end of the journey in the afterlife. No one was actually at that level except the Creator and some of the angels and guides. No one even knew how many there were. No Plane 3 souls, or trainees spending time on Plane 4 and 5, were allowed to interact with angels and guides, so it was a mystery. There were books in the afterlife for those who were interested in reading and understanding the overall hierarchy. Most people were so thrilled and busy with their afterlife lives that they rarely did any research at all. Why mess with perfection? It was all good here. Just enjoy.

It was all fine with Dani, too. The hierarchy of the afterlife made sense. Choices could be made, and Dani had made hers. She knew the drill. Having been involved in many transitions since she became an Elite, she was careful to focus on the mission and do what she needed to do to complete it successfully no matter where or what the circumstances were. She had encountered many Plane 1 demons and incredibly evil entities. While they would terrify the average crossed-over soul, Dani was confident that she could handle them one way or another. She always had; however, this next job was going to be a bit different. She was going to retrieve one of the very men she believed was involved somehow in her murder. They had a connection, albeit a connection that had not by any means been dishonorable or strange to Dani at the time. They did share a love for Friesian horses, and her beloved Cole was the offspring of his Grand Champion stallion Magic. While they were both involved in the horse world, they also both worked in real estate. He had become very powerful, loved his new girlfriend Charlotte, and was not interested in dying. Not that most people would be. But because he was wealthy and had means far beyond most people, he actually thought he could prevent his death from happening.

He had done some minor studies on the occult and was interacting with some dangerous characters through his business associates, who he believed had ties to entities that were able to invade the Earth plane at will and accomplish great feats and miracles, like preventing death and curing illnesses. He was working hard to find a way to live forever, and he was running out of time. Dani of course knew this was not possible, and it would only make things more difficult for him and his transition to try and interfere with his destined timeline.

The entities took advantage of the weaknesses of the human soul and reveled in the process of making them think they could actually beat death. They were extremely dangerous, and no human was a match for these evil creatures. They would inhabit an accommodating Earth soul and do their dirty work. The Creator of course was well-aware of their diabolical attempts to change the Universal time algorithms. It was a wonder that they even tried. It rarely worked. And when it did, there were remedies on the other side to fix the mass disturbances that they created. Yes, it was a mess to deal with. But it was fixable. They rarely won. And almost all the souls they interfered with were ultimately forgiven and happy to find the peace in the afterlife that they so desperately sought on Earth. Dani never understood why the Creator didn't just wipe out Plane 1. There was a reason, of course, and one day she would get the answer. All in due time.

So Dani would have to step in and clear the path for a safe and timely transition for her subject. Dani was ready.

Was Earth ready for Dani?

# Chapter Five

Levi's transition had been peaceful and expected. He had suffered for many years with a debilitating and terminal disease, and when his time came, it was a relief for his grief-stricken family, because he had been in pain for so long. They watched him suffer and both dreaded and prayed for his passing. He was a kind and gentle man in his late 40s, and he had been a friend and father to two amazing children. He had watched their lives for years from the confines of a wheelchair and a bed. He was ready to go. Ready to be rid of the chair and the frustration that plagued him every single day. He was done seeing the looks of pity and sadness on the faces of all whom he came in contact with. He had read every book and seen every movie he could have ever wanted. He was done. He was tired. And when he finally passed, it was with sadness and relief.

Upon arriving after death, he had been reunited with his mother and father, other distant relatives, and friends. All the animals he had known and had never forgotten were there to greet him. It was like a giant family and animal reunion. Tails wagging, lots of meows, and a few he didn't recognize. Eventually, they would all become clear to him, and it was heartwarming to think that he could be with them again. The pain of each and every loss was gone. Only happiness and love surrounded him.

His only son, Jeff, had recently joined him on Plane 3 due to a tragic automobile accident. While he was overjoyed to see him, he knew the agony and sadness that had been left behind. His son also knew that his father was about to partake in a dangerous adventure that could end his life…again. Only this time, it would eliminate his ability to ever be an Assistant again, let alone a Plane 6 Elite, and he would stay on Plane 3 for eternity. Not really a bad thing, but not the exciting existence he wanted.

He had lived a cautious and illness-dominated life on Earth for years. He was unable to do so many things. While his mind was strong, his body had failed him. His disease had progressed quickly in the last two years of his life, landing him in that wheelchair, barely able to do anything to take care of himself. It was frustrating and emasculating, and he had definitely been losing his zest for life. Thoughts of suicide began to dominate his thoughts. As he looked back, he was now hungry to make up for that horrible time by evolving and reaching the highest honor he could: Plane 6 Elite. It was a lofty goal, but he knew that with hard work and lots of determination, he could do it. After all, he was healthy now. There was nothing to stop him.

This new assignment would help him determine whether or not he would pursue that endeavor for sure. It was what he thought he wanted, but he also had gained much wisdom on the other side and was slightly open to the idea that this might not be something that he would or should pursue going forward. Things could change on the other side. His wife might come home to him and have a completely different plan or idea for him and his family. He would see about that when the time came. Levi hoped that he would still have many more assignments to complete before that would even be an option, and he wanted his wife and daughter to live full and amazing lives on Earth.

Right now, this was his intention. He would be working with the best and the most beautiful and intimidating being he had ever seen, Earthly or otherwise. Was this crazy? He thought on it often. Things were so different on the other side. Magical and amazing things happened every day. Did he really need this extreme adventure? Was it worth risking death—again? After pondering the idea for about 30 seconds, yes, he decided. The more extreme the better.

His son Jeff was worried. He too had heard about the strange Plane 6 beings…and their super powers. While he was comforted that his dad would have serious protection from an Elite, he knew that there was a chance that something could go wrong. But of course, if death was the worst thing that could happen to his dad, they both knew that they would still be together eventually on Plane 3. He simply didn't want his father to experience pain or suffering of any kind ever again. He was in such a wonderful place now. Jeff knew that Levi wanted to be an Elite and knew his reasons for it. It made sense, and he was proud to know that his dad was doing a great thing and that he was making great strides after such a miserable existence on Earth. He deserved to be healthy, stimulated, and challenged, and Levi assured him that there would be plenty of reinforcements if things went sideways. Levi was not allowed to talk about the specifics of the assignment or say anything about the Zengats to anyone. He felt that if his son had seen a Zengat, he would definitely not be so worried. Levi wasn't sure how he would describe one of those creatures anyway. He had always been an animal lover, especially dogs. His loyal companion Sparky had been by his side until the end. The thought of Sparky meeting a Zengat shot a chill down his spine. One bite. Sparky would be toast. But there was nothing to worry about. Sparky would be fine, and he would soon join Levi and his son on Plane 3. It had been seven years since Levi died, and Sparky had only been four years old at the time. He was getting old, and it wouldn't be long now. His son looked forward to seeing their furry friend again soon. There were no Zengats on Plane 3.

Unlike Earth, on the other side, thinking about someone experiencing death was not such a bad thing. It was all part of the overall plan that the Creator had for everyone. While it might seem unfair and tragic at the time, there was always a reason and a purpose to every human death on Earth. And if Levi really thought about it, being dead was not so bad. Not bad at all. Inhabitants of Plane 3 also knew they would soon be reunited with every being they had ever loved or cared for— and some that they did not. That was the beauty of the afterlife. Things got figured out. Things made sense, and even enemies became friends. Time in the afterlife was filled with activity and pleasure. Rejuvenation. Higher learning was available to everyone who passed over. You could find answers to all kinds of questions that on Earth only seemed like fantasy or myth. Levi reveled in the new experiences and the ability to do whatever he wanted to do physically. He could also do all the things now that he couldn't do with his son while he was on Earth. They tried to make up for lost time on Plane 3, and it filled their moments with joy and gusto, something only realized on the other side for Levi.

Time was not the same in the afterlife as on Earth. It all seemed to run together without skipping a beat. All of the agonizing elements of waiting for certain things to take place on Earth just wasn't an issue. There was some waiting of sorts, but it was different. Everything blended together seamlessly. The pain and trauma of the Earth life was very real, and the memories were as well, but the two places were so different. It was easy to focus on time in the afterlife and let Earth and its traumas play out on its own, even if it was your own family. You knew they would get through it and end up in the most wonderful place in the universe. After some time, Plane 3 humans would be able to understand all the dealings and questions that living on Earth had created, and knowing that they would see their animals and loved ones again eventually was the greatest comfort of all. Levi assured Jeff that it would all work out. He would not be gone long, and he would surely have some great stories to tell when he returned.

Jeff would wait patiently, which would not be long. He would also try to find out as much as he could about the strange Plane 6 Elites while his father was off on his transition adventure. Because Jeff had just recently crossed over, he was still getting the lay of the land in the afterlife. He was smart, and he knew he could access information in a number of ways. The libraries and halls of knowledge were massive and could be intimidating, but he was excited and energized to delve into any information he could find on the mysterious and elusive super beings that inhabited Plane 6. His dad wanted to be one of those beings someday, and Jeff wanted to know everything.

Levi and Jeff parted with a huge hug. They would both be busy. When things weren't busy, Levi had a special place in the afterlife where he spent a lot of his time. You could be alone or with as many people as you wanted when you wanted. When he just desired to meditate or be solitary, he would seek out his spot by a beautiful turquoise-blue lake under a giant maple tree. The colors in the afterlife were magnificent. Earth would seem like a drab version by comparison. Yet while on Earth, one might think that some places were the most beautiful that they had ever seen. *Just wait*, he thought with amusement, *you just wait*.

As Levi sat by the lake and prepared for his assignment, he thought about Dani. What was her Earth story? She was so amazing and powerful. What was she like as a young Earth girl? Hard to imagine at this point. He knew he would probably never know the whole story or even part of it. Dani wasn't the warm and fuzzy type for sure, and he knew she wasn't going to have a heart-to-heart talk with him any time soon. She was so tall and stunning. What would people think about these two mismatched people hanging out together? At his height, lean and ordinary in appearance, there was no way he could ever look or be as cool as her. They would be a match made in heaven but definitely not in the traditional sense. They weren't supposed to be a couple on Earth as their cover, just friends or associates when in full view of the public. But the general idea was to stay out of the public as much as possible. Just focus on the person who was their subject and any other Plane 1 beings that might impede that person's transition.

Earth had become more progressive in the seven years since Levi had left, and all kinds of strange people pairings were perfectly normal; however, Levi was pretty sure that Dani could potentially draw unwanted attention. Would she be recognized as another type of being? No, she would look human, but even after the ten years that she had been gone, people wouldn't forget someone as striking as Dani. Hopefully, there would be no one in proximity who could identify her. After all, she was not a celebrity of any kind that he knew of. As soon as he had that thought, it occurred to him that she was so magnificent, maybe she was indeed a celebrity of some kind or a famous athlete. That could cause some issues, for sure. He could see the papers now: "Local celebrity mysteriously comes back from the dead." She would have to be careful not to draw attention to herself. Levi was pretty sure that she had already thought about it. If there were any concern about her being identified, surely it would have come up during Levi's briefing.

He would be nowhere near his wife and daughter while they completed their assignment on Earth. As much as he would love to see them, he knew that was not going to happen. Ever. Not until they found their way home to him. He would wait. It was amazing how time in the afterlife was so full and didn't allow for a lot of dwelling on the past. It was all about going forward and becoming more enlightened. While fond memories existed, you didn't have to be sad about them. You could keep your mind focused on seeing them again. It would all work out in the end, and everyone on Earth had a destiny that needed to be fulfilled to cross over and go forward with their long-term enlightenment.

He was ready to go.

It was getting close to the time that Levi and Dani would be leaving for the Earth plane. Levi had his scan card from The Ancients. He simply inserted it into his small master computer, and the information was all there to access or memorize as to how they would get to their destination and what the plan was in general to cross over their subject. Like most things in the afterlife, it was simple and seamless planning and execution. There were several launching pads, so to speak, for the hundreds of Elite 6 beings to use for transitions to and from the Earth plane and anywhere else they wanted to travel, including other planets and solar systems. That too was one of the reasons that Levi wanted to become an Elite. Travel. Elites had access to the Universe, and Levi wanted to experience it firsthand. On Earth, he had never gone anywhere. He had barely left the house, let alone traveled the Universe. It was mind-boggling, and he hungered for the opportunity.

As he thought about the future, he checked himself. Back to reality. He would have to complete this and many assignments before that would ever happen. This crossover would be the first step in the process, and he would need to focus hard on the task at hand. The man they were to transition was going to be a hard case indeed, but Levi was curious as to why this was so dangerous. This was his first assignment as an Assistant, and some of the details were curious. He knew he would have to play some of it by ear, the free will part of the equation, which was always a part of everything afterlife-related. It all seemed like a fairly cut-and-dried task with someone as capable as Dani at the helm. Having thought this, he realized that there were probably all kinds of things he did not know or understand as a new Assistant. The nuances of the game, so to speak. It was a Class X Transition, and that guaranteed trouble of some kind. It might mean big trouble if they wanted Dani and the Zengats to handle it. He would go with the flow and try to be a very quick study. During his training, he had been introduced to the Plane 1 entity possibilities as well. Knowing that one or more might interfere with this transition, Levi was even more determined to be there for Dani and to get them both through unscathed.

As an Assistant, of course, it was his job to help Dani fit in and to do Earthly type tasks for her as needed. He knew that the Zengats would never be far away if needed. They just appeared out of nowhere, it seemed. Levi thought it was disturbing and really kind of cool at the same time. To have those lethal animal weapons at your disposal, well, at Dani's disposal, was amazing. He was pretty sure that they would not take any commands from him, although the thought of that was crazy. To have that much power at your beck and call. Awesome. And dream on.

Levi studied their subject, Frank Kenning, who was a well-known businessman and drug dealer amassing a fortune from the market of a new and illicit drug that was not available even on the black market. He was the only way to get this synthetic drug, and the demand was high. He had a small but powerful group of people who supported his drug business and served as informants and business covers. In the beginning of his newfound success, he wanted to change the trade completely, which would make him the most powerful drug lord in the US. But things were changing fast, and Levi knew that Frank's life had definitely been a wild ride. He had recently met a woman who seemed to be a major influence in his life. Things were getting complicated for sure. He wondered about Frank's life and the man himself.

# Chapter Six

Frank was 6 feet 3 inches tall, devilishly good-looking, and appeared to be in fabulous shape. At 50 years old, his black hair was thick and wavy, barely a grey hair in sight. He looked like a model right out of the pages of Esquire magazine. You would never know that he was struggling with a terminal illness. He had the money to do everything possible to keep up appearances, but the strain and reality of his sickness was beginning to take its toll internally if not so much externally. He had begun to limp slightly, and it was making him angry. This was not the image of a powerful man like himself. He was desperate to cure his illness by any means possible. He diligently worked to create a super drug to eradicate his disease, but it was taking too long. He was running out of time, and he knew he was way out of his league, trying to cure cancer.

He felt that he would have to go to extreme measures to prolong his life, with the help of some people that he would not otherwise have anything to do with. Although he was embedded in the drug world, he didn't really fit the typical profile of a drug kingpin. He wanted to preserve his pristine reputation and believed he could have both: tons of money and a normal life.

Frank had built a huge empire through drug dealing, manufacturing, and distributing with the help of his college roommate, Richard. He then became a successful real estate investor to launder some of the drug money and to hide his not-so-legit other business. He built a majestic property, with horses and pastures that colored his 1000-acre estate. His barn was full of expensive horses, and his stallion was in demand. He would breed him sparingly, and any of his descendants were a hot commodity. Frank was known for his horses, and people were calling on a regular basis to purchase from him. John Davidson, Dani's father, was not among them. Magic was his baby, and the magnificent animal was at the end of his breeding days. Frank was happy to be able to put his big boy out to any pasture of his choosing. No more breeding, and no more new horses. The thought of leaving his beloved horses without him to care for them after his death weighed on him. He had made a plan for them but did not want to implement that plan. Not any time soon.

Frank had led a charmed life. Well, for a while anyway, and now except for the terminal illness that plagued him. He had been diagnosed with a rare cancer of the brain. He was still completely lucid and high-functioning, but he knew that it was only a matter of time before the effects of his cancer would begin to create real problems for his business and his life in general. Love and family had eluded him for the better part of his life, due to his line of work and inability to stay grounded. Although pursued by gold-digging women in throngs, he had recently met someone who was beginning to have an undeniable impact on him and his way of thinking about life, love, and his drug business.

Before he met her, he had turned to horses as his outlet for love and caring. They gave him peace at times, when he felt that he might never have it again. The one woman he had married and loved earlier in his life had died of another devastating type of cancer. He never wanted to go through that again, and he was one of those people who thought he would never love again. That was it. Kristen was it.

But life had a different plan for Frank. While working on a project for his real estate business, he was unwittingly paired with a beautiful woman buyer who had taken his breath away at first sight. Try as he did to ignore her and not get involved, it was inevitable, as she had the same immediate attraction to him. It was kind of love at first sight, and he knew this was going to be another serious affair. Keeping his illegal business practices hidden from her would be a challenge. She had fallen hard for him and wanted to be involved in all aspects of his life from his business to his horses.

She was smart and knew the real estate world very well. She herself had bought and sold several expensive properties and was enjoying her life and the rewards that having money had given her. She grew up around horses as a young girl and quickly fell in love with Magic and the rest of the horses on his property. While he tried to do business as usual, Frank was distracted by his new relationship, and it was having an effect on everything he did and thought. She was also starting to wonder about some of his strange friends.

Charlotte was changing him, and her hold was powerful. She was a very principled person. Someone who would not tolerate his underworld empire. He knew that she would never stay if she found out what he was really up to. Frank would have to rethink his business and everything else if he was to continue his relationship with her long-term, however long that might be. She was bright and worldly and wanted a peaceful, carefree life, which was not something that Frank was completely focused on right now. He had been somewhat honest with her about his illness but held back the part about it being terminal. He led her to believe that he was trying a new experimental drug that would slow the process and eventually cure the problem altogether. She trusted him and was thrilled that he would soon be healed and healthy. When they met, he had no signs of illness, and she was convinced that he could do anything he set his mind to, including getting well. She envisioned a long and exciting life with Frank, and she would be there to support him through any challenges that might come their way.

Frank knew that getting caught in this big lie could mean the end of his love affair, and he so desperately wanted to be with her. He needed her to get him back on the track of being a regular good guy. Not a seedy drug kingpin. The drug business and making more money was falling way down on his list of priorities. It was more important to stay alive to be with Charlotte. That life had never really suited him, and his partner Richard was also weary of the possible consequences of mingling with so many unsavory people. He too liked the money, but there had been some frighteningly close calls with guns involved. Richard was feeling like they were now in way over their heads. Richard and Frank had more money than they could ever spend. Get out now. That was the new mantra.

All the more reason to get that special drug created to save Frank. Richard was the only one whom Frank had told about the terminal aspect of his disease. They had talked long and hard about what would happen to the business if Frank died. Obviously, Richard would be in charge, but Richard too had a woman in his life, and they were considering having a child. It seemed to be the right time to let it all go. Their synthetic drug was in high demand, and they would have to make a plan to shift the business away from them completely. Make a clean break, if that was even possible. They were well-known in the underground community, and it wasn't always a pleasant place to do business when they had to. They saw themselves as white-collar drug dealers, not the creepy scumbags that they sometimes had associated with. Though deep down, they both knew that they were drug dealers. Plain and simple. The ugliness attached to it had taken away any thrill of the two "college" boys looking to hit it big and live a carefree and fun life. Things were getting dangerous, and they both wanted out.

It was difficult to distribute without the help of some questionable men. Felipe was one of those men. While he was always available and did a good job, his associates were sometimes scary as hell, and Frank refused to deal directly with any of those people. That was Richard's job. Felipe had the inside track on everything involved in the business. Except the money. Frank was not about to let him in on that level. He was paid well for his participation and seemed quite happy to support Frank and Richard in whatever they wanted and needed. Greed has a funny way of creeping into one's psyche. Against his better judgement, Frank had to tell Felipe that he was ill, but not terminal, and that he wanted to do whatever he could to get better. Felipe appeared saddened to hear this news and assured Frank that he was willing to do anything to help.

At least, that was what he wanted Frank to believe. It didn't take long for Felipe to begin thinking about how he could turn this sad situation into a windfall for himself. It wouldn't be long now before Felipe would start viewing things differently and start the wheels turning to take care of Frank. And not in a good way.

When Frank finally came to Felipe in need of something, some kind of a drug, to slow his disease, it was obvious to Felipe that this illness was much more serious than

Frank had let on. Felipe now suspected that Frank might be dying and that the business was going to be changing.

Felipe wanted to ensure that his stake in the operation was solid. He had visions of taking over and becoming a powerful drug lord. He had worked hard and long for Richard and Frank. He deserved to be well-compensated. To be taken care of. He began to dream about the money and what it could do for him and his family. If Frank was eventually going to die, he would have to get something in writing before that day came. The drug formula at a minimum. He would need to get Richard out of the picture also.

Felipe went to his cohorts and asked around. He needed someone who could be highly convincing and could create some kind of potion or pill that would make Frank believe that he was getting better for a short period of time. Something that would actually kill him before he had time to give everything away. To the wrong people.

Frank was visiting doctors on a regular basis, so the pill or potion would need to be something that was not easily detected during routine tests. Felipe had no idea what exactly Frank's disease was, and he surely didn't know what it would take to fool the doctors and get rid of Frank. Now he knew that he would also have to get rid of Richard, because Frank would not want Richard to be left with no business or major cash flow. It would have to be taken care of before Frank actually died. The timing would be critical. Frank seemed to be doing pretty well and not even looking or acting sick at all. There would be time to get it done.

Richard would be the first to go, maybe in an accident or something that would not be traced back to Felipe. Because of some of their shady dealings, Frank would think that Richard's death was drug business-related, and he would not look to blame Felipe, his trusted partner. That would be the easy part. People died all the time due to the nature of that business.

Frank was another story. Things were moving quickly, and determining the right method of death for Frank was crucial. Felipe would have to go to one of his darkest and sleaziest associates for the answer to that one. He knew just who to talk to. CJ.

CJ was a person whom no one really wanted to talk to. He had lived a strange and hermit-like existence for as long as Felipe could remember. He knew that this guy was the one person who had connections to mediums, tarot card readers, and such, and his time spent amongst the dark arts and the people who performed them was significant. He knew how to get anything you wanted. Even if it killed you. He really didn't care. He was interested in money, and everything that he provided came at a big price. Generally, people were desperate if they came to him, and he knew he could milk it to the max.

Felipe and CJ were not what you would call friends. But CJ liked Felipe, and he knew that he was connected with lots of money via Frank Kenning. They rarely saw each other, as Felipe wasn't thrilled with all of the hocus pocus stuff that CJ constantly spewed at him whenever they met. When they did meet, near CJ's home, this time was no different. CJ was getting older, and he was getting more demanding. His stories were as boring as ever. Felipe wanted to get to the purpose of the visit. He needed a potion, pill, or doctor who could kill Frank Kenning in a short amount of time and make it look natural. He explained to CJ that Frank was already sick, and his death could easily be contributed to that illness if it played out convincingly.

Felipe had money but assured CJ that when the deed was done, there would be more money than they had ever dreamed of. Though Felipe didn't buy into all the things that CJ was doing, he did not want to be on the other end of a disgruntled CJ. He knew he could end up dead.

CJ thought about what Felipe's needs were. He quickly came up with the name of a woman who had amazing powers and could conjure demons if she had to. *Demons*, thought Felipe. He just couldn't believe that was possible. Things he had heard made him wary of dealing with anyone not from this planet. It sounded crazy, but CJ assured him it was doable. Felipe wondered why they needed such a person. Couldn't someone just create a pill, and that was that? It seemed so simple to Felipe.

CJ made it clear to Felipe that to fool the doctors and Frank, it would take a very special poison to get the job done. The woman would pose as a healer and new-age wellness professional and would administer the potion over a short period of time in the form of a tea. Frank would become ill and lose his battle with his disease, while it looked like he simply died from complications. She would conjure a demon if necessary to complete the plan. Give her more power if she needed it. Felipe had no idea what he was talking about, but he knew that CJ had been successful in many death contracts, and he would have to trust him to get this job done. Demon or no demon.

Felipe and CJ were not aware that their timing could affect the Universal algorithms unless the time of death coincided exactly with Frank's destined death time. Of course, The Creator knew that this could happen if it was left up to

Felipe, CJ and some evil woman. Thus, Dani would have to step in to make sure things went according to Universal time.

Felipe and CJ had no clue that Frank was destined to die relatively soon and that if they just waited long enough, he would be gone, but Felipe wanted to make things happen sooner than later. The thought of all that money was making him crazy with greed. So he and CJ devised their evil plan. Frank would be so thankful to Felipe for finding a cure for his disease that it would be easy to play him and get the job done. Andromeda, would stay at Frank's house and ensure that he got his daily dose of death. If anyone or anything tried to stop her, well, she would call in an otherworldly entity and make quick work of things. Andromeda was well-versed in demonology and conjuring. CJ quickly set up a meeting for Felipe to meet her. Felipe was not looking forward to the meeting. He just wanted to get on with it.

Felipe returned to CJ's house the next day, and there she was, in all her bizarre glory, waiting to meet Felipe. She looked like something out of a Halloween movie. She was dressed in black from head to toe. All she was missing was a large, black wart on the end of her long, skinny nose. A bit scary, Felipe thought, and that was something that he was concerned about. Frank's girlfriend Charlotte wasn't going to be thrilled with this whole exercise, and he knew he would have to come up with a reasonable yet effective explanation. Charlotte was spending more and more time at the house, and this strange-looking woman lurking around wasn't going to be well-received, on so many levels. Still, CJ convinced Felipe that it would work. Andromeda would be introduced as a new-age healer. It was something that people were getting used to. A hip, new thing. If it could actually heal the man, they would be all for it, regardless of what the impressions were.

Felipe decided to go forward with the idea. Andromeda would give Frank a cup of spiked tea every morning. It would be laced with poison but nothing that would be detected by Frank or his doctors. It was a special blend conjured from the demon that she was communing with. A demon that was ready to take over her body and step in if necessary to keep the plan in motion. CJ neglected to mention that to Felipe, for fear that he would call the whole thing off. All Felipe knew was that the poison would cause Frank to start losing his faculties and to be vulnerable to signing anything they put in front of him. Death would soon follow with a final dose.

Felipe was ready to move forward. He would have to set up Richard's accident soon. The poison was set to take effect in five days. Soon, Felipe would be the most renowned drug lord in the US and beyond. He would have the secret formula to Frank and Richard's special synthetic drug.

Life would soon be very good.

Felipe was anxious to get out of there. The old woman was giving him the creeps. He left to go meet Frank, wondering the whole time how this was all going to turn out. Poisons and the like were not his usual operating procedure. Felipe was more into quick and dirty killings. Unknown to Frank and Richard, he had already been involved in several murders unrelated to their business. He had a side business of his own. Something that they would never find out about. He was building his connections and paving the way for the day he would take over Frank's holdings. Now it was happening, and it would be so much easier than he ever dreamed.

He had taken advantage of their naiveté and was able to fly under the radar. He knew that Frank was vulnerable and that he would take advantage of that. Felipe told Frank about this special woman healer who had access to all kinds of things that could help make him well. He convinced Frank that this was the only way to guarantee complete success and to get the health and happiness he really wanted. He explained that this amazing woman would be able to reach beyond the confines of Earth and utilize special powers to create total healing, even if it meant dealing with some unsavory beings. Frank actually didn't even want to know the nasty details; he just wanted the cure. It all sounded strange and unbelievable, but Felipe had assured him that this was not a joke. There were ways to do things that Frank could not imagine, but it would be costly. Frank was not the type to just let a plan go forward without complete control; however, it was clear that he was just beginning to lose control physically and mentally, and he would have to rely on trusted friends and associates to get him through this tough fight. One thing was certain: he had the money to pay for it.

He agreed to let the woman stay at his home, and he would come up with a convincing explanation for Charlotte. He would tell her that this "new-age" healer was going to give him the best chance to get better and that it would all be over soon. She would stay at the house and hardly be noticed while she was there. No real inconvenience.

Charlotte loved Frank and agreed to go along with his plan to get well, even if it meant having another woman in the house for a while. Charlotte was used to spending lots of time in his home and interacting with his two dogs. They loved her and followed her everywhere, unless Frank was around, and then their loyalty quickly shifted to him. They were there to protect him, and they were always on the job. She wondered what they would think about this other person.

Charlotte liked having the big house to herself when Frank was not around, and having someone else there was going to be interesting. She hoped that she would not have to interact with her too much. But then, maybe she was just a sweet little lady who wanted to be of help. It was a lovely thought.

The woman Frank had hired to facilitate the creation of the drug that would save his life needed to make it happen soon. Felipe had drawn from his underworld connections and had guaranteed a cure for his disease by introducing him to a local healer who would save his life. Someone who was supposedly able to conjure otherworldly spirits who held the answers to the cure. Frank could not wrap his head around any of it. He tried to keep from thinking about what he could do with a drug that cured cancer. After he was cured, he might have to consider creating a super drug. Save the world. *One step at a time*, he told himself. He wanted to live. That was the priority.

Andromeda would create a concoction for him to drink over a short period of time, which would attack the disease quickly until it was eradicated. Frank was willing to try anything at this point. His doctors had told him that the cancer would begin to manifest its effects soon, and he could be bedridden in a matter of months, death not being far away.

While he and Charlotte enjoyed a seemingly carefree existence, it was far from that for Frank. He would now have to change everything. Possibly sell the business to begin a new life with her. A legit life. No illicit drugs. Just clean living. He knew that Richard would be happy to get out of the business. They were making so much money that stopping suddenly would barely have an impact on their finances. Frank also knew that if he could create a legitimate cancer drug, it would mean fame and even more fortune for both of them. He would wait to tell Richard about the possibilities after he was cured.

Felipe knew that Frank would never turn the business over to him. He was a lower man on the totem pole, and he was only important now because he had set Frank up with the woman who would prolong his life, maybe even cure him. He knew that Frank would feel obligated to him but not enough to share a major stake in the business. He didn't know of Frank's plans to eventually get out of the drug business altogether.

It was a business that Frank should have avoided from day one. He flew under the radar of the police by maintaining a totally legitimate business in the world of real estate. He bought and sold multimillion-dollar properties with ease. He was a natural. He didn't need to go into the drug business at all, but greed has a way of finding its way into one's soul. Even though he personally never used drugs, he saw the relatively easy path to millions and could not pass up the temptation. He hired master scientists to develop amazing drugs that the young and wealthy clambered to get their unsteady hands on. These drugs were not for the typical street dealers or buyers. This was the top of the line. Mysterious and wicked. Through word of mouth and secret networks, he dominated the market and was making a fortune that only the most successful drug dealers could dream of.

There were plenty of buyers who wanted a piece of the big action, but Frank was not interested. It was a small operation. He liked it that way. His associate, Felipe, was a good solder but not capable of actually running the business. Frank and Richard did that. Felipe made sure that the deals were done and that distribution was in line. He was a glorified gofer.

This was something that Felipe was tiring of. He would figure out a way to get the business interest put into his name before Frank inevitably died, as Felipe had no intentions of saving him. The sooner he was gone, the better. Felipe knew he could run the business and make even more money. He was willing to deal with people that Frank and Richard wouldn't even consider. He was obsessed with the idea. He needed to get Frank to sign some paperwork, wait for the "new drug" not to work, and he was home free.

He would rule the drug world and be the envy of all those who had written him off as a flunky. He would be the man. He could taste it.

He couldn't stop thinking about how wealthy he would be. As soon as he found out that Frank was sick, he had seen his opportunity. Frank would never know what happened. It was a great strategy. Again, best laid plans, they say.

# Chapter Seven

Frank Kenning was so rich yet so ill. At this point, he simply wanted to live. Just live. His lavish lifestyle was something to dream about for Levi, having lived a simple life as a lower-middle class man with few expensive trappings or extras to speak of. Most of his money had gone to pay medical bills and to provide for his family. He was lucky to have worked for a company whose benefits covered costs associated with long-term illness and care. His family was cared for, and he found comfort in knowing that after he was gone, they would be okay. It was strange to think about it all now. How were his family members doing? He could find out through various afterlife channels, but he knew it was not the afterlife policy to dwell in the past or on your Earthly life. It would only interfere with your progress going forward, and there would be plenty of time to catch up with loved ones when they arrived home. He would pass between Plane 4 and Plane 5 for his Assistant training, then return to Plane 3 where he spent the rest of his time. His son Jeff was a gift to have with him now. He would be with his wife and daughter soon enough. He enjoyed the time now with his parents. Afterlife was good. Real good. He was also looking forward to seeing his beloved dog Sparky.

Levi was looking forward to spending some time amongst the rich and infamous as well, a world he did not know or understand, really. The mega rich did things differently, and the Earth was changing with regard to the kind of power these wealthy people could wield. On Plane 3, wealth literally had no importance. It was a level playing field, so to speak. It was all about who you were and what you would do going forward. While the afterlife was abundant with great works of art and beautiful palaces and views for miles, it didn't all have the same meaning as on Earth. It was true reality. All things were and could be accepted, even amazing concepts and places that on Earth were completely out of reach for most people. On the other side, if you had an interest, you could explore it, have access to it, and have your questions answered. It was extraordinary. It was powerful. Levi was in heaven. Literally.

Frank Kenning, like Levi, was now struggling with a life-threatening disease. This was the one thing they did have in common. Levi knew that Mr. Kenning had engaged the help of some strange and powerful people to help him live longer, possibly rid himself of the disease entirely. It was crazy to think that money could actually buy one man a cure for a physical death sentence. And as it turned out, it wasn't possible, at least not on the Earth plane, without a little help from above. That was a highly complicated matter indeed. Something Frank would have to wait to understand.

Crossovers took mere seconds in Earth time. That was… normal crossovers. People who were dealing with the dark arts made things more difficult, especially if they had conjured a demon or other unsavory entity to assist them. Those entities did have power, and only someone like Dani could take them on. Because these entities originated from the other side, only beings from Plane 6 could get rid of them. Levi knew that he was not capable of that, but he felt that Dani and her Zengats would make quick work of them. It was an assumption he was comfortable with. He reminded himself that he was also protected by the Zengats while he was on the Earth plane. Though it was reassuring, he hoped it would not be necessary. That would mean that things had probably not gone well. What would he do if anything happened to Dani? Would those giant beasts still protect him? He would try not to think about it.

The overall intention was to approach the subject, Frank, find out what otherworldly beings he was engaged with, determine what their powers were, and then time the transition with the natural death that was going to occur for this man whether he liked it or not. Any other entity within range of the man would have to be dealt with...prior to the natural death. This was obviously the problem. There was a natural order of things. An Earthly deadline, so to speak.

Levi finished looking at the scan and felt that he knew as much as he was going to know until they actually descended to Earth. Which was going to happen very soon. He would meet Dani at the designated launch site, and they would go from there. The taking-off point was no secret to the Elites, but Levi was given confidential directions and was not allowed to discuss them with any other souls. He would bring a computer, phone, money, etc., so that they could assimilate into the world below without being noticed.

Right.

*No chance of that happening*, he thought as he saw Dani in the distance preparing to set out on their short journey to Earth. Levi could only imagine what Frank Kenning would think about her when their paths crossed. This was going to be interesting, and Dani would be disposing of some creepy entities, no doubt. Levi shuddered a little at the thought. He had worked hard to prepare for this journey, and he was going to do the best job he could do. No matter what.

As Levi approached, he could see Dani watching him closely. Was that a smile? No. It was a look. One that he would come to know quite well during the journey ahead. And what was she wearing? Her silhouette was stunning. He realized as he got closer that she was wearing tight jeans and cowboy boots. Thank goodness. The green leather jumpsuit would have made things challenging, to say the least. Her auburn ponytail gleamed in the light. She was undoubtedly a vision. No blending possible. Even in jeans. He would deal with it. Levi himself felt ordinary, even more so when standing next to Dani. He also wore jeans, "dad" jeans, to be exact. Nothing sexy about Levi. It was pointless to try to measure up to the likes of his partner. He would be the basic Earth guy but ready for action.

They greeted each other in the most friendly and awkward manner he had ever experienced. Dani was not big on small talk. That was okay with Levi. He was going to take all this seriously, not worry about becoming buddies with Dani.

Just do a great job and move on to the next case. They stepped onto a round, glowing crystal platform barely large enough to accommodate both of them. There was an eerie quiet for a few seconds, and then suddenly, they were on their way. Through time and space. It was magnificent.

Brilliant colors and swirling images engulfed them as they seemed to float next to each other. There was no sound. Just shapes that could only be explained as ethereal and nonconforming. Before Levi knew it, they were standing at the end of a long, country road. It was like awakening from one dream and entering another. The Earth's sun was beginning to go down. It was a clear summer's eve. He was back on Earth. The air felt heavy, and it took a few seconds to adjust to the reality of where he was.

He was a dead guy, standing on a road on Earth. Nothing weird about that. He thought that as long as no one knew he was from the other side, he was just another guy in dad jeans walking down a country road. Levi took a deep breath and prepared himself for whatever might come his way. And his way it was coming.

# Chapter Eight

As they walked along the desolate road on their way to their destination, Levi was struck by the calm and beauty of the open and expansive pastures that flanked him on both sides. Still, it all seemed so dull compared to the scenery on the other side. There was no comparison. In the afterlife, the trees were greener and the sky was more brilliant, and now it was like some kind of Earth déjà vu. He had been told that it would take a short time to acclimate to the Earth's atmosphere. Levi hoped it would happen soon. After feeling so light and healthy, this was a reminder of a struggle on Earth that he preferred to forget. He wondered if they were going to be walking the whole time. The heaviness of his partially human body was starting to feel weird.

No car or driver services? He and Dani had not really communicated since they arrived, and he was exceedingly careful with his thoughts. He knew that their destination was not too far ahead in Earth miles, according to the GPS. They would not enter the Kenning estate this evening. They would just get the lay of the outlying area and town.

Dani was in charge, and she would manage the time and activities at all times. *Easy*, he thought. He would just go along and wait for instructions. *There was a plan in place. Nothing to really worry about yet*, he told himself. Try not to look at her or think loudly. He knew that there possibly would be otherworldly entities at play. Dani was calm. So he would be calm.

They had only been walking for a short time when she suddenly stopped.

Levi instantly had a bad feeling. He knew they were not at their destination, and Dani thinking of varying from the task at hand already was concerning to him. She was looking into the distance, where an old farmhouse and barn loomed in the twilight. There were lights on inside the big, old barn, and he could not see or hear anything out of place. This was definitely not the Kenning estate or any part of it. What had stopped her?

Dani looked at him and simply said, "Follow me."

*Oh, boy, here we go*, he thought. Darn, did she get that thought? If she did, she wasn't interested in his thoughts right now. She was clearly on a mission of some kind, and Levi knew it wasn't part of their assignment.

He was not going to try and stop her, of course. He was going to go along and see what this was all about, knowing that it could mean trouble for them. Him. With The Ancients. While he knew The Ancients were not watching their every move during the transition, it seemed plausible that they would ultimately know what happened on Earth. Levi did not want to do anything that would jeopardize his ability to become an Elite, yet he knew he could do little if anything to stop Dani. He struggled to keep up with her as she marched quickly toward the barn. She was after all about 5'10". Walking through uncut grass and huge weeds that seemed to be about four feet high, they soon approached the old building. Dani walked directly to the pasture on the west side of the huge wooden structure. There in the moonlight, Levi could see the outline of a large white horse lying on the ground not moving or even breathing, it seemed to Levi. Dani rushed to the horse's side. The animal was barely alive, and she knelt down beside the suffering mare.

As Levi got closer, he could see blood on one side of the horse's head and a large 2 x 4 lying next to her...covered in blood. This was not good...not for the horse or the person who had done this.

Dani was furious. Her body was now emanating some kind of weird aura that was reddish in color. Levi had never seen anything like it. He knew this was bad. She was really angry.

Levi backed away as Dani cradled the horse's large head in her arms. She was saying something that Levi could not understand. After several minutes, he watched in amazement as the horse began to move. Dani stood up and moved back. The massive horse slowly got to her feet, and they stood facing each other. With what could only be explained as pure love in her eyes, the mare blinked as if, to say, "Thank you." Dani's aura calmed to a light pink, and she immediately guided the horse to another pasture and made sure that she was safe. Levi was frozen in place, simply watching it all unfold before him. He knew she was communicating with the horse but could not understand what was being said. The horse was calm and slowly walked into the pasture and away from the horrible bloody scene as though nothing had happened. But something had happened. Something really awful.

Levi was in awe. He looked at Dani as she briskly walked past him, looking straight ahead. He tried to pick up on her thoughts, but she was in some kind of mission mode, and he could only stand by and watch. She was headed for the barn, where sounds of laughter billowed from the large open doors. It sounded like a party going on. *Party's over*, Levi thought.

Three weatherworn and scruffy men sat on several hay bales stacked together in front of an empty stall and were going on about how they had taught that bitch a lesson. They each had a beer in hand and were enjoying the thought of just having beaten the poor horse to death over something that they didn't like.

They were dressed in dirty jeans and overalls, and one had an old cowboy hat barely balancing on a head of gnarly gray hair. They looked like they had been drinking for a while.

Probably their whole lives.

The old barn was filled with a dingy yellow light, and the two large wooden sliding doors at either end were wide open. Looking down the barn aisle at one end, an old farmhouse with tattered curtains and faint light peeking through could be seen in the distance.

There were several stalls in the barn with various horses that appeared to be hiding. Hay was stacked randomly, and various farm tools and equipment hung on the walls like a menagerie of functional junk.

Levi was having a hard time keeping up with Dani, as she seemed to glide faster and faster toward the open door. She turned quickly, looked at Levi, and said, "Other side."

Levi took that to mean he should go to the door at the opposite end of the barn, so he quickly ran around the building, trying to avoid horse poop and gopher holes, stopping at the entrance and looking directly at the men sitting and laughing.

The first thing they saw was him. Looking toward the door, they stopped laughing and, almost in unison, said, "What do YOU want?"

Before Levi could answer, Dani entered the other open barn door and stood facing them.

At this point, they were totally confused and not sure what to think or do. Dani walked slowly into the barn. Either the men were completely speechless, or Dani had put some kind of spell on them. They just sat and watched, mouths open, as she slowly walked toward them. Levi decided he would not move and just watch, as Dani was clearly in control. She could easily make quick work of these yahoos.

She was now directly in front of them. They were large men, and they would have been intimidating to another man under normal circumstances, let alone a woman. But as Dani stood before them, Levi could see the sweat begin to form on their foreheads.

She just stood there and stared at them for what seemed like eternity.

Finally, one of the men spoke. He looked at Dani and angrily asked, "Who are you, and what do you want? Better get the hell out of my barn and take your puny little sidekick with you before I show you—"

As the man began to stand, Levi could feel a cold breeze engulf him. Suddenly, a Zengat was moving past him and slowly walking toward the men. *Puny sidekick, huh? Well, we'll see about that.* Levi smiled.

The man sat back down, and Dani said nothing as the large beast came within six inches of the man's face. The three men froze. They were horrified and huddled tightly together on one hay bale like little girls at a horror movie.

The Zengat stopped and sat. Its hot breath now showering the man as he feared for his life. Levi was enjoying every minute of this exercise. The same could not be said for the three men, who were now visibly shaking.

Dani suddenly spoke. "You have beaten an innocent horse. You clearly have no respect for the precious life of that beautiful animal. The horse endured much pain because of you.

This is not the first time that you have been abusive. What do you have to say for yourselves?"

*This was gonna be good*, Levi thought. *What could this guy possibly say, and with a giant black dog from hell breathing down his neck?*

The man stilled. He didn't know what to make of the big black creature and wondered who these people were and how they knew he had beaten the horse more than one time. The other two men were like frozen statues, occasionally looking at a nearby shovel as though trying to find a way to protect themselves.

Mustering every bit of testosterone he had, the man turned to Dani and said, "Look, I don't know who you are...or why you think it's your business what I do to my horses. She had it comin'. She stepped on my foot, 'bout broke my toe. And if you think you are going to do somethin' about it, well —"

A small boy, roughly 10 years old, appeared at the opening that Dani had entered, and he wasn't alone. Beside him was a large black dog. A Zengat. The boy could see that there was something happening in the barn, but he was excited and yelled to his dad, "Look at this cool dog I found, Dad! Isn't he great?"

Again, not a sound from anyone. As the Zengat next to the man was breathing down his neck, he was horrified that another one was sitting next to his young son. His boy was petting it. Unexpectedly, the huge animal laid down and rolled onto his back so the boy could scratch his large, pink belly. It looked like the man might have a heart attack right then and there. Even Levi wasn't sure what to think at this point. But he knew that Dani would never hurt a child, so he just looked on and enjoyed the show.

Dani glared at the man. "You have committed a serious crime against an animal. You must pay."

The man, who was trying to keep an eye on his son and Dani and the dog next to him, softened. "Look, what do you want? I may have been too hard with the horse. But I can't do anything about it now. What's done is done. I promise not to hit another horse ever again. Just get that thing away from my boy, and we can forget this ever happened."

"There is no forgetting. And you must pay for your crime," Dani said as she flashed her green eyes at him, which were now intensifying in color, almost glowing.

With that, Dani turned to the boy and raised her hand. The Zengat stood, and with its long black tongue, gave the little boy a big lick on the side of his face. The man looked paralyzed. The boy giggled and said, "Dad, isn't he pretty? Can we keep him? Look, Dad! There is another one by you! Cool! They're twins!"

Dani said to the boy, "Sweetheart, they are my doggies, and they have to come with me. But he was very happy to meet you, and maybe he'll come for another visit someday." She looked at the panicking farmer, adding, "You should go to the house now, dear… right, Dad?"

The man tried to smile and urged his son to run along to the house. He told the boy he would be along soon, though clearly unsure he would make it out of the barn alive.

The little boy gave one last hug to the big animal, whose eyes had now turned a ruby red as it glared directly at the man. The boy then ran quietly into the night toward the house.

*Now what?* the man wondered. What horrible punishment was he in for from this strange lady and her even stranger dogs? It was all so unreal.

If he only knew.

Dani turned her attention back to the three men. "You will not speak of this night to anyone. If any of you ever lift a hand in anger to another animal, or human, you shall have an unwanted visitor."

The Zengat sitting next to the man began to growl, his brown eyes turning a radiant red as he displayed a mouth full of jagged white teeth with saliva dripping down onto the man's pants.

As Levi leaned against the door, trying not to chuckle, he could see the three men were completely distraught and crying uncontrollably. "We are so sorry. Please, don't kill us. Please. Please don't hurt my boy."

Dani looked at Levi and instructed him telepathically to retrieve the horse.

As he hurried from the barn to find the horse, he suddenly realized he had never even pet a horse, let alone retrieved one.

He grabbed a rope hanging at the entrance to the barn and walked into the pasture where he saw a large, white shape slowly coming toward him. Now, he was scared. What was he to do? This wasn't Plane 3, where all animals were gentle and approachable.

Dani began to speak to him. *Relax. Just gently put the rope around her neck loosely and guide her to the barn. She will follow.*

People were always telling him to relax.

Like a miracle, the beautiful animal let him put the rope on her, and together they calmly walked toward the barn. He would remember this moment, and he planned to spend time with the horses on Plane 3. They were everywhere and easily accessible to any human who wanted to touch or spend time with them. He was looking forward to it.

The Zengats backed away from the men and sat quietly at both entrances to the barn.

As the men looked on in amazement, they saw the horse they thought that they had beaten to death enter the barn, seemingly healthy and with no signs of ever being harmed.

Levi led the horse into the barn and stopped. The other horses in the barn began to stir with excitement. The large white horse was fearful of the men. That was clear. They were now all crying and appeared to be remorseful. Dani approached the horse and said something telepathically to her. The horse walked directly over to the very man who had almost killed her. She nuzzled his neck, and the man melted into a pool of sadness and regret. He reached out his hand to the animal, and with tears in his eyes, he said he was sorry and that he would be the best horse owner there ever was. The horse became calm, and the man was holding her head in his hands. It was clear to Levi that this man—these men—had learned their lesson and that they were truly remorseful. The threat of the return of the Zengats would be impossible to forget, but it was clear that Dani had helped change their hearts.

Dani had done her job here. As quickly as she entered the scene, she was gone.

As was Levi. He had no clue where the Zengats went, and he wasn't going to ask. Seeing the Zengat rolling on the ground and getting its tummy rubbed. Seriously? There was clearly a lot he didn't know about Zengats and Dani. He had to admit it was all exhilarating. He hoped The Ancients didn't find out about their little side adventure.

He was beginning to really like Dani...and those Zengats.

# Chapter Nine

Levi and Dani had not done a lot of talking since arriving on Earth. The details were worked out, and there really wasn't a need for conversation regarding their plan until it was actually in process. He wanted to discuss the whole horse incident but felt that Dani would talk about it if she wanted to. He was unsure how to interact with her and was gaining so much respect for her that he wanted to get closer, to be friends. Was that even possible with a Plane 6 Elite being? He figured out that she wasn't always reading his thoughts. Only when they were intentionally corresponding. He would have to be careful. He was developing a comfort level quickly, and he knew that he would be helpful to her when needed. The puny sidekick comment still bothered him, though. He would try to be more substantial somehow.

They were continuing along the road together in silence when Dani suddenly began to cry. *Oh, no. What do I do?* He had no idea, and he had no idea why she had become emotional. Was it the horse? The horse was fine, and she had scared the crap out of those farmers. It was all good. Right?

Levi felt sympathy for her, and he just had to ask. "Dani, are you ok?"

She stopped in the middle of the road, the moonlight reflecting off her beautiful silhouette. It was difficult to ignore how gorgeous she was and to not think about it. Even though it was distracting, he had to remain professional. He sensed that for Dani to become emotional, it must be important.

She turned to him and spoke. "The love of my Earth life is near here. I can feel him. But I cannot approach him, nor should I. I do wish I could see him, though, just for a moment."

"Is he part of our assignment?" Levi asked confused, wondering if he had missed something in the briefing. Surely he would have remembered that Dani's man was going to show up during their transition process. "Does he live around here? Aren't we on our way to Frank's general neighborhood?"

Avoiding Levi's question directly, Dani stopped crying and became somber. "I took us a bit of a roundabout way. I honestly did not plan on the horse. I am extremely sensitive to animal distress. I have no tolerance for animal cruelty of any kind. We need to stop for the night in the town just ahead of us. I will explain when we get there."

Levi was anxious to hear what she had to say, and at the same time, he was concerned there could be more potential animal rescues during their short time on Earth. They had a job to do and a specific amount of time to get it done. It was his job to keep her on task, and at the first sign of trouble, he had just gone along with the whole thing. Idiot. This was a test for an Assistant. To keep the Elite on task. It just wasn't that easy. While he knew that the animal intervention was not part of the overall plan, he had wholeheartedly agreed with everything she had done to help the horse. It was amazing to watch, and she had transformed three lives at the same time. What could The Ancients possibly find wrong with that? Levi figured he would find out when he got back. He would try to be more demonstrative. More confident in his approach with her.

He would trust Dani for now. He could now see the faint lights of the town ahead and wondered why they hadn't just rented a car. Although he was feeling a bit lighter, and more Earthly, he wondered what other physical changes he might undergo over the next few days.

They walked into the town, no talking and no telepathy, and immediately Levi had the sense that it was not going to be a simple overnight stay. So far, nothing about this assignment seemed basic or simple. As they entered the small town, it was strangely quiet, and he was thankful for that, because it might have appeared just a little weird to see the two of them causally walking into town from wherever, for whatever reason. There were not many people around and hardly any cars or noises anywhere. Not even a dog barking. *Thank goodness*, he thought to himself. Dogs might mean another critter rescue.

It soon became clear why there was no activity and that there was something happening at the town hall. It looked like just about the whole town was there.

Dani was now walking briskly and seemed determined to get to where she was going without stopping to check out any of the goings-on. As usual, Levi had to basically speed walk to keep up with her. As they moved past the front entrance to the old building with large windows and glass doors, he could look in and see people sitting and standing in the crowded main room. It looked to Levi like a fairly raucous crowd. The man at the front of the hall behind a podium on the stage was trying to quiet them down.

Almost simultaneously, Dani looked into the room as they passed by, and the man looked toward the front window. He stopped talking. Levi was watching the whole thing and noticed that the man had stopped abruptly. He seemed to be focused on the front window, and Levi realized that he was actually looking at Dani. At about the same time, Dani looked into the room and immediately became flustered. She walked away so quickly that Levi had to run to try and catch up with her.

"Dani!" Levi yelled to her as she disappeared quickly into the dark. He stopped when he heard a door slam behind him, and he turned to see the man at the podium standing on the front step, desperately looking in all directions.

It suddenly all clicked. This was the guy. Dani's guy. Oh, boy. Awkward. That had to be incredibly weird for both of them. Especially him, since she was technically dead. As for her, she was most likely expecting or planning to see him at some point.

The man was frantically looking for the beautiful girl he had just seen pass the window and wondering how he was going to find her. Levi was frantically trying to figure out where she had gone and wondering the same thing. The two men looked at each other. The man ran up to Levi.

"Did you see a woman with long, reddish hair pass by here?"

Levi would have to lie. That was not something you could do on Plane 3; however, he was on Earth, and lying was highly common.

Levi looked at the man and said calmly, "You know, I didn't, actually. I wasn't paying attention to anyone as I walked along. Is there something I can help you with?" He was dying to know what the man would say.

"I thought I saw someone I know—knew. It was her. I can feel it," he said with an excited tone in his voice. "But it's impossible. Not possible. Sorry to bother you. Have a good night."

"No problem. Same to you," said Levi as he watched the dejected man turn and slowly walk back to the hall.

Levi's heart sank. It was him, all right. The pain of loss was clearly evident, and Levi knew what that felt like. He and Dani would need to talk, all right. That was, if he could find her.

He headed in the general direction in which she had fled, and he looked everywhere. It was getting darker, and the streetlights were of little help in those tucked away, hidden areas when you were looking for a woman in dark clothing, with dark, red hair.

Just when he was about to give up, Dani stepped out of the shadows and said, "Let's go. The hotel is just a few blocks away."

She knew what Levi was thinking, but she wasn't ready to talk. Again with the walking. This whole episode brought back memories of real life on Earth, and he began to think about his wife Ann and daughter Jessie. *Stay focused, Levi,* he thought. *Stay focused.*

Levi had been given Earthly currency and had everything available to him, including his tablet, phone, etc. Dani would be needing none of it. Until tonight, there had been no need for any of that. Except, of course, to rent a car. When they finally checked in to a chic boutique hotel in the quaint little town, they could look forward to nicely appointed rooms and every Earthly comfort they needed. Separate rooms were in order, and Levi worried that he might not be able to talk with Dani before they turned in for the night. On Plane 3, you could sleep if you wanted, but it wasn't necessary. It was actually more like meditation. Settling your mind, refreshing your body. But this was going to be a long Earth night. You could only meditate for so long when you had a million thoughts running through your head.

He did have a little work to do regarding the assignment. He wanted to play his role with the utmost clarity and intelligence. He was in another world, literally, and dealing with the likes of Frank Kenning meant that he would have to come across as a savvy businessman with expertise in the real estate field. Something that he had none of. The good news was that all the basics had been planned and figured out for him. He literally just needed to look and act the part. Be convincing, charming, and attentive. He would focus on that tonight. They had to deal with Earth time. So the hotel stay was for convenience.

They checked in, and Levi watched the night attendant stare at Dani the whole time. He wondered how the guy was able to finish the transaction, he was so distracted. It was clear the attendant didn't think that Dani could possibly be with a guy like him. Only business, for sure. Depressing.

He then directed them to the staircase. There was no elevator in sight. It was an old but beautifully refurbished building. They each took their key and went their separate way. She must have known that he wanted to talk, but he would leave that up to her. He had no intentions of upsetting her any further or prying into something that would undoubtedly be a touchy subject.

Levi's room was comfortable and a bit frilly, in his opinion. If he had wanted or needed to sleep, this would be a soothing place to do that. White lace curtains and red velvet-covered chairs added to the charm and ambiance of the room. Not his style but elegant. He decided he would sit in the beautiful, overstuffed chair, put his feet up, and start reviewing his plan for the next day.

But before he could get to the chair, a quiet knock at his door gave him a start. He opened the door, where Dani, appearing forlorn, slowly entered his room.

She walked over and faced the window, looking out into the night as she spoke. "His name is Adam. He was the love of my Earth life. Still is. Things were wonderful with him. We were planning a wedding and getting our lives together and making arrangements. We were young and thought the world was ours. We were going to have a big ranch with lots of animals. Lots of horses. He was working as an equine veterinarian, and I was beginning my real estate career. It was all so perfect. So simple.

"I joined a real estate group in Grant City, and Adam was getting new clients daily. We were even in the process of buying the ranch that we had both dreamed of, and it was where we were going to have our wedding.

"I was leaving the office one day to head home when my boss asked if I could meet with him and the owner of a new house that he wanted me to represent. He was excited and said that this could be the listing of a lifetime for me and for the business.

"I asked him why he didn't just take the listing himself, and he said that the owner had specifically asked for me. I asked who the person was, and he said a wealthy businessman named Tyler Hoyt. I had never heard of the guy. And I said so. Frank just said that it was a nice referral and not to look a gift horse in the mouth. I didn't get it. Why me? But I was young, and I figured it was a great opportunity, so I agreed to meet Frank and the owner at the residence. I called Adam and told him I would be a little late. Well, that was an understatement. I never made it home," Dani said with a sigh.

"As I pulled into the driveway of this massive mansion, I noticed that the property looked somewhat vacant. Frank said that the owner would be there. A green sedan was parked in front, but it didn't look like it belonged to anyone who would live in this house. And it wasn't Frank's car. I decided to go ahead and see who was home and introduce myself."

Levi thought, *Frank? The Frank that we came to transition?* He just stared at Dani and waited anxiously to hear more.

"I rang the doorbell. No answer. Odd, I thought. Maybe he was not there yet, but who did the car belong to? There was no lockbox, and I didn't have a key, because I thought I was meeting the owner there. It felt strange. It was such a beautiful place. A dream home. Massive columns in front and huge trees on a perfectly manicured lawn.

"I wondered where the owner was and where Frank was. I decided that if he didn't answer the door soon, I was leaving. I called Frank but got his voicemail. No point in standing around at an empty house. I really wanted the listing, but I was anxious to get to Adam and to get on with our evening.

"Just about the time I had that thought, one of the two front doors slowly opened. An elderly man dressed in a black suit, like a butler maybe, stood there. He seemed to be agitated and frail. I asked him if he was the owner, and he just looked at me with a blank stare. He was white as a ghost.

"I asked him if he was all right, and suddenly another man stepped around him and walked directly towards me carrying a gun.

"'Shut up and get inside. NOW,'" he screamed at me.

"I was stunned. What was happening, where was the owner, and what was this man going to do?

"As soon as I entered the house, it was pretty obvious that this guy was robbing the place. Expensive items were strewn everywhere, and the large man holding the gun seemed to be in a panic to get out of there. The older man was barely standing and appeared ready to faint or have a heart attack. I ran over to help him, and the man with the gun shot me. Just like that. I fell against the older man, and we both crashed to the floor. The pain was horrible, and I think I was passing out when I heard another shot.

"I looked up and saw my sweet dog Rolly standing in front of me wagging his tail. I was suddenly in a place of brilliant light and warmth. Rolly was leading me someplace, and I was happy to follow. I looked back and saw the old man crumpled on the floor as the scene began to fade away. I was confused at first, and then I was on my way….and, well, you know how the rest of the story goes."

Levi was mesmerized. Seeing Dani now, it was hard to believe that anyone or anything could have taken her out.

She had died during a home invasion robbery, it seemed. Just an innocent person in the wrong place at the wrong time. It made Levi sad to think about it. He didn't know what to say to her. Wow…sorry you had to die like that? That was awkward at best, and he felt that this was a conversation that only people who had died could actually have. Weird.

He did understand how Adam must have felt. It was obvious by the look on the poor guy's face that he had never really gotten over it. Dani had been brutally murdered, and Frank Kenning must have been involved. Levi wondered where Frank had been and why he had not come and saved her. He had a lot of questions, but he knew this would be a touchy subject on so many levels.

They both stood in silence for what seemed like a long time. All Levi could say was how sorry he was for her loss. Of life. Dani was a woman of few words, but she had taken the time to tell Levi about her friend Adam and her death. Levi felt even closer to her now.

He knew there was much more to the story, but Levi was not going to push it with her. Not tonight. They said an awkward good night to each other, and she walked slowly out of the room.

Levi was exhausted both mentally and physically from all of that Earth walking. He would now meditate or maybe get some Earth sleep and be ready for whatever tomorrow would bring.

# Chapter Ten

In the early hours of the next morning, after a restless night, Levi was fully immersed in meditation and was startled by a knock at the door. Expecting to see Dani, he was surprised to see the hotel clerk standing before him. He had a note in his hand and handed it to Levi, who promptly read: Meet me at the coffee shop.

He thanked the clerk and gathered his things, knowing he would not be spending another night at the inn. Since he had never seen Dani's handwriting, he assumed that the note was from her. Who else could it be?

He quickly made his way to the only coffee shop in town it seemed and looked around for Dani. She was not there. Now what?

He decided to take a seat and wait. Had something happened during the night? Was something wrong? Or were they just getting started on the day?

In all her heavenly glory, Dani walked into the coffee shop. There were only four other people there, and all four of them practically spit their coffee out when they saw her. She was that gorgeous. Levi was now used to the way she looked, but ordinary people would not see someone like this every day, or ever, in person. Maybe on a fashion runway or in an action movie, but not in a little coffee shop in small-town Hudsonville.

Levi had to smile. It was quite comical.

Dani, on the other hand, was serious as ever, and Levi knew that this was the beginning of the transition period. Their bonding session the previous night was all but a memory. He immediately focused and said, "Good morning, Dani."

She gave him the slightest smile and asked him to arrange for a cab.

A cab? No more walking? This was great news! Levi quickly made the call. As they left the coffee shop, Levi was again amused by the reactions of the patrons trying to pretend they were simply enjoying their morning joe. Dani didn't seem to notice and was soon at the curb pacing. In short order, a car arrived. It was a beautiful day, and he knew this was the beginning of the plan in earnest. He was excited and nervous at the same time. Dani didn't seem to be nervous about people recognizing her. She may have allowed for that and would never show herself at times when it might be a problem, of course, except when she stunned Adam.

Although the basics of their assignment were set, he knew that things could get chaotic at any time, especially if the Zengats and evil entities were involved. None of it seemed possible in this quaint little town. Zengats and evil demons. Who would have thought?

The taxi pulled up, and Dani immediately got in but not before she stopped and looked across the street. Levi also looked in that direction and saw a man mostly hidden by a large tree quickly disappear behind the tree. Dani got into the car, and Levi knew it was him. Did Dani know? Of course she did. What was she thinking? She could not show herself to him. It was another facet of Dani's being that Levi would have to adjust to. She was in charge. She had to know the consequences of seeing Adam and what kinds of problems that would cause for her, him, and the Universe. Levi would focus on the task at hand, and he didn't want her to read his mind, so he immediately opened the laptop and studied the estate of Frank Kenning.

The car pulled away, and Levi couldn't help but take another quick look to see if he could find the man. He was gone. He felt that this part of the journey was not over. She wasn't saying anything, and Levi was not going to bring it up, as usual. She had to know that Levi had come face-to-face with Adam. She didn't mention it, so Levi would follow suit. As the car pulled onto the main road, Levi had a sudden feeling of foreboding. He knew that there could be some dangerous entities involved, and he was entering some unknown territory. Even with the Zengats available, he had to admit he was a little scared. He looked over at Dani.

She was smiling as she looked out of the car window. She looked at him, and said, "I will need to get the feel of the property. I want to make sure that every entry point is current and noted. There are two guard dogs. I will deal with them immediately."

Levi wondered what exactly that meant. Again, he knew that Dani would never hurt an animal. He now wondered what she would do if she were confronted with a seriously badass guard dog or two. But what was he thinking? Nobody had really seen badass dogs until they had been confronted by Zengats. He didn't need to worry.

Mr. Kenning was on a death timeline. Something he could not control. No matter what he thought. That timeline needed to stay in check, and Dani was going to see to it that it did. They had several Earth hours to be in place at the time of the transition. They had already spent some of the time just getting used to the Earth plane and spooking Adam, not to mention resurrecting a large horse. As the mid-sized car wound through the countryside, Levi wondered what he would encounter first. Vicious guard dogs, fiendish demons, or Frank Kenning? Levi would be the point man and would enter the property under the guise of an appointment with Mr. Kenning to work on a lucrative real estate deal. Dani would check out the exterior property and assess the situation. Dani's ability to become invisible would come in handy when things got sticky, another thing that made it almost impossible to kill her, even on the Earth plane.

She had so many weapons at her disposal. Still, when invisible, her aura could be detected by high-tech security cameras, so she would have to be strategic in her movements. To a human, this would just seem like a weird camera problem, but if a conjured entity could see her aura, it was a different story. It was explained to Levi that the woman helping to save Frank's life was not an entity. She was an Earthly medium who could conjure entities to mess with Frank's mind and give the old woman powers that she would not normally have on Earth. And those powers would be strong and not easily dealt with by Plane 5 souls who transitioned regular people. She could become possessed by an entity or demon for short periods of time if she felt threatened.

It was all pretty out-there to Levi. Frank was going to die one way or another; this medium was only trying to change the timetable. But that was enough to bring in the big guns. To bring in Dani. The Universe would not be happy about a lengthy stay of death for Frank, and Felipe and the medium needed time to get Frank to sign papers and turn the business over to him. It wasn't going to happen with a change in the will. There would need to be specific plans for Felipe to become the new head of the drug empire. It would take a little time, and the medium would use all kinds of tactics to get Frank to sign papers. A morning tea was just one of those ways. It was slowly dulling his mind and making him more open to suggestion. His girlfriend Charlotte was even beginning to notice the change in him. His date with death did not coincide with the medium's plan for him, which was why Dani needed to make things happen on time and to keep Frank from signing any paperwork. That was not in the destiny plan for Frank either.

Because Richard was also ready to leave the business, they had determined to whom they would hand the business for a big price. Frank had taken care of everything in his new will. His beloved horses and dogs were to be left to Charlotte. She would also inherit his vast real estate holdings and the home that they were to share. He hoped that he would be there with her, but things were getting confusing and strange to him. His headaches were getting worse, not better, and he felt the need to spend as much time with Charlotte as possible.

It seemed like his horse Magic sensed that something was going on as well. He had been agitated and not wanting to eat for a few days. Frank was worried about him and had called his veterinarian, Adam Pruett, to take a look at him. Adam knew, of course, that Dani's horse Cole was Magic's offspring. While Adam never really understood the whole story surrounding Frank's part in Dani's death, it was rumored that the break-in was drug-related and that Frank might have known the killer. The killer was never apprehended, and the murder went unsolved. Adam had tried for years to find the killer and bring him to justice, but the system hadn't worked in his favor, and it had soon become a cold case. Adam was never sure of Frank's involvement, if any. Frank had given lots of business to Adam over the years, making him profitable beyond his wildest dreams. Out of guilt, perhaps.

It was all so complicated. Now Adam was trying to help the man he wasn't sure he could trust and help the horse that played a part in making Dani so happy. He knew Dani would want him to help Magic, but unfortunately, Adam knew it was improbable he would recover. The blood work revealed a bad infection that would be difficult if not impossible to treat. Frank was devastated but held out hope that a miracle would save his beloved horse. Adam did his best, and they would have to wait and see.

Levi's meeting with Mr. Kenning had been planned via The Ancients and a connection that they had on Earth. There were Plane 5 humans who were available to help The Ancients from time to time with just these sorts of tasks. They had no super powers, and they were trained not to disclose their assignments. They simply entered the Earth plane for short periods of time, did their jobs, and returned.

A large commercial development was being built near the small town. It was a convenient ploy for Levi to step into to discuss a deal as a big investor. That always got Frank

Kenning's attention. Levi would scope out the home and find out who was inside, he hoped. But after looking at photos of the house, he knew there was no way he could check every room in one visit. Not even close. He had a floor plan, etc., but there were lots of little nooks and crannies that he would not be able to inspect. He did not have the ability to see entities or demons—that was Dani's thing—but he would get a good read on Frank, and he did have the ability to sense when someone was possessed or just plain out of place. They knew that they were looking for an older woman who could conjure evil entities at will. Levi was simply to assist, not actually do anything crazy like try to take out a being from Plane 1. *Just as well*, he thought. He would leave that to the Zengats and Dani.

And he would try very hard not to get in the way.

Frank was scheduled to die at 1:30 p.m. Earth time on Tuesday. He would suffer a massive heart attack due to complications related to his long-time terminal illness. It would happen in his barn. Levi was aware that there were many animals on the property. He had seen the horses as they drove up, strolling in the majestic pastures that surrounded the estate. He kept that in the back of his mind as he asked the driver to stop and drop Dani off about a half-mile from the entrance to the home. He told the driver that she wasn't feeling well and needed to walk for a while.

She quickly exited the car and turned to Levi. "I will meet you here in one hour." That was it. No good luck. No words of encouragement.

He was starting to get Dani. Cool as she was, it was comforting to know that she was in charge. He trusted her judgment and hoped it would all work out. It appeared that she trusted him. It was a good feeling, and he was inspired to make this transition go as planned.

Dani had no doubts. She was looking forward to the challenge. After many Class X Human Recoveries, she was well aware of the obstacles that were awaiting her. Seeing Frank Kenning again would be emotional for her. She knew who her killer was, and she knew that Frank really had had nothing directly to do with her death. Because he was friends with the owner of place at the wrong time. But there was something else at play. Why had she been requested by the owner of the home to be the realtor? And why had Frank not been there? Perhaps it had been some way of getting back at Frank for something?

Dani was aware of Frank's other business. Through her research, she had discovered that he was dealing in illicit drugs and was making a lot of drug lords angry. He was not the typical drug lord, and he clearly didn't understand that they were ugly, desperate, and evil people who would do anything to make a point. He was highly intelligent but also naive when it came to dealing with these people. He was actually way out of his league. Had Dani's death been the point they were making to him? Had they taken her out to get to Frank? It weighed on her. It was all so messy. But the killer would get his due, and this was not the time for Dani to focus on her death. It was Frank's time.

She also knew that Magic was going to die. While devastating for Frank, she could only imagine the grand reunion that would take place between Magic and his sweet boy Cole. It would be marvelous.

Dani was ready to check the place out. She quickly walked toward the estate, fading into the surrounding landscape like a golden fog. Grasses moved and rustled beneath her feet.

Game on.

Within minutes of Dani leaving the car, Levi could see the massive estate in the distance. This was the kind of home he could not even imagine, except for having seen a few on those rich and famous shows on TV. He never dreamed he would be spending time in one, let alone making a business deal with the owner. He was well versed in the art of this deal, and he was ready to get to it. The car slowly pulled up to a massive iron gate with an ornate letter "K" taking up most of the space. Immediately a man's voice came over the intercom at the left side of the car.

"May I help you?"

Levi leaned across the driver and answered, "Yes, I am Levi Janson. I am here to meet with Mr. Kenning. I have an appointment."

There was a brief pause, and the ornate gates slowly opened. It was a little like a Plane 3 arrival scene. Majestic and awesome.

As they continued up the tree-lined driveway, Levi looked for any sign of Dani. She was probably there by now, and he felt confident just knowing that. While he did not see her physically, he knew she was probably in stealth mode, and he would be able to see her aura. He envied her. It would be so awesome to be invisible. Yet another reason to become a Plane 6 Elite.

# Chapter Eleven

As the car pulled up to the enormous white mansion before them, Levi could see a man already standing on the front landing waiting to greet him. He noticed that the driver seemed to be in some kind of trance, just staring at the huge building in front of him like he was looking at one of the world wonders.

Clearly, he had never seen anything like this before. *Join the club*, Levi thought. And just wait until he saw what was waiting for him on Plane 3! This was nothing. Levi turned to the driver and told him to park the car and that it might be 45 minutes or so. He also told him not to leave the car for any reason. The driver seemed sufficiently intimidated by Levi and the whole scene in general. He would stay in the car.

Dani had entered the estate from a hidden gate at the back of the property. It was locked, but she was able to pass through and easily enter undetected. She couldn't see any dogs, but she knew that they were there somewhere. If they couldn't see her, they would be able to sense that she was there. That might be a problem, because she did not want to harm any animals, and she did not want the Zengats involved. The property was several hundred acres of pasture and rolling hills. Dani had a slight déjà vu moment. Frank Kenning had done well for himself. Dani knew that some of his business practices were aboveboard, of course, but the one that wasn't was extremely illegal indeed. He had dealings with some shady characters, and at least one of them was someone whom Dani had known on Earth. She tried to stay focused, but she knew that if she encountered that particular man, it would be difficult not to take action. Action that would get her into trouble with the The Ancients. She would deal with that when the time came, if it ever did. Right now, she was closing in on the house, and she was curious about how things were going with Levi.

As she moved closer to a large window at the back of the home, she suddenly heard a low growl emanating from behind her. Another growl chimed in. She knew they could not see her, but they knew she was there. Two large, black, furry Bouvier Des Flanders dogs stood next to each other looking at her as she turned around slowly. This breed of guard dog could be deadly. She had encountered one when she lived on Earth while showing a property. They looked a lot like giant stuffed animals, even looked cute, but she knew that when they were on the job, there was nothing sweet and fluffy about them. These two were confused, and she wanted to keep them from actually barking if she could, because they would draw unwanted attention to her location. Dani knew she would have to show herself and use her powers of persuasion with them.

As she slowly came into focus, the dogs suddenly stopped growling. Dani was communicating with them telepathically, and she was doing her best to let them know that she would not hurt them and that they could relax and be on their way. She was no threat. They stood completely still, staring at her. They were not growling, but they were not leaving either. They seemed to want to be with her, and as she turned to move toward the house, they followed right behind her.

Dani would have to become invisible again, and she now had two big, hairy animals shadowing her every move, something she was used to. She was pretty sure she had even seen their cropped tails wagging.

Under other circumstances, she would have loved to pet and interact with them, but this was serious business, and she would have to manage with her new companions. As she faded into invisibility, the dogs were not fazed. They were her new best friends, and they were going to stick with her. Not exactly what she had planned, but she would deal with them tagging along.

By now, Levi was deeply into his business dealings with Frank and seemed to have things under control. The deal was totally legit on paper, but that was about it. If Frank knew he was being scammed, things would set sticky real fast, but because he would be dead in less than 24 hours, Levi knew that there was little chance of the deal going sideways. It was strange not knowing where Dani was exactly, and as he looked through the large window behind Kenning's head, he saw two large dogs walking along, seemingly checking the outer perimeter of the house. That was odd. They must be extremely well-trained to be able to literally walk the perimeter of a house as part of their guard duties. He wondered if Dani had encountered them. Before he could have another thought, Frank Kenning asked him if he wanted to take a walk with him. Levi knew this would be his chance to check the place out.

Before he could answer, an old woman wearing a bizarre and quite unattractive black outfit entered the room seemingly out of nowhere and approached Mr. Kenning. Frank excused himself and walked with her through a door and out of sight. No one else entered or left the room, or the house, it seemed, during this interlude.

It was quiet, and there was a smell of incense filling the air. Levi looked around and was amazed at the beautiful artwork that adorned the walls. He was taken aback when he noticed a photo sitting on a nearby table. As he walked closer, he realized that the woman in the photo was Dani. She was sitting on a black horse in what appeared to be a corral next to a barn that looked a lot like what she had described as her childhood home. Before Levi could gather his thoughts, Frank entered the room.

"So sorry about that. I have not been feeling well, and I needed to take some medication. You are lucky if you have your health," he said with a sigh. "Living with a disease can be challenging. Be thankful that your long life is still ahead of you."

Levi was not sure what to say to that. He knew exactly what it was like, but he wasn't about to get into that conversation with this man. He had a job to do, and he was almost done for today. They had made their deal. Both Frank and Levi were pleased with the impending partnership that they had just agreed upon. Levi only wished he had really been able to do deals that lucrative. When he was still alive, of course. They were finishing up, and he would soon leave the magnificent home. Levi could not help but look again at the picture he knew was Dani. Frank clearly had some kind of affection for her and maybe some guilt about what happened. Levi would never know. Asking about it would raise suspicions, and that was not something that Levi could or wanted to do.

As Levi walked toward the front door, the woman who had entered the room earlier was ascending the giant staircase that seemed to go on forever. Levi watched her move eerily up the stairs, almost floating. She suddenly stopped and looked back at him as though she knew he was staring. Was he seeing things, or were her eyes changing color? He felt a chill run through his body. Did she know who he really was? She was definitely not your average human. Oh, yeah, she was possessed, all right. Dani would have her hands full with this one. She appeared to be the only obstacle for Dani, as had been suspected. Because he didn't have full run of the house, he would never know who or what else was lurking around.

He had heard about the evil entities who came from Plane 1. This woman was not from there, because she was human, but Levi felt that she was headed in that direction. Once on the other side, Plane 3 beings were not to interact with souls as they made their way through Plane 2. The intense reprocessing they were dealing with could be brutal, depending on their deeds on Earth. The length of their stay on that lower level was not set in stone. She would definitely be a 2, and depending how this all went, maybe a 1, if that was even an option.

The woman then turned her stare back towards the stairs and disappeared into the upper level of the house. Levi turned his attention to Mr. Kenning and tried not to appear rattled by the old woman in black. Levi knew that the she was not Frank's good friend, family member, or girlfriend. His research had been clear that the man was single and recently involved with a woman named Charlotte. A very attractive young woman. Levi knew who this peculiar woman was. Her name was Andromeda, and he was interested to see how her encounter with a Plane 6 Elite would go down.

Frank had not felt the need to introduce the woman to him. Levi was relieved. He really didn't want to make direct eye contact with her or with any entity she might be harboring. It made his skin crawl.

Frank looked at Levi and cheerfully said, "Let's head out to the barn for a few minutes, and you can meet some wonderful friends of mine."

This would have to be a quick trip. Time was getting tight, and he needed to meet Dani precisely when she expected him. As they walked through the home, Levi took it all in. It was magnificent. Nothing seemed odd or out of place. An older gentleman approached them as they entered the kitchen.

"Jesop," Frank said, "this is Levi Janson. We are heading out to the barn. Levi, would you like anything to drink?"

Levi said that he was fine, and they continued to leave the house and head to the barn. Levi wasn't about to drink anything made in that kitchen.

Jesop seemed like a regular guy. Nothing suspicious there. The usual butler garb and mannerisms. At least, Levi assumed that was what it would all look and be like if he were wealthy beyond his wildest dreams.

As they walked through the lush grounds and manicured pathways to the beautiful building that was the barn, Levi could not help but think that Frank would be dead in a matter of hours. Yet it was difficult to feel sympathy for him, knowing that he would be entering a place where anything was possible, where bad deeds were examined and dealt with, and where it was up to you what would lie ahead. The opportunities were endless. Much of what he had done and was dealing with would be washed away from his thinking at the appropriate time. That was the good news. The bad news was that if you engaged negative and evil entities while on the Earth plane, there would be some minor hell to pay, in a manner of speaking. Nothing like the fire and brimstone you might see in a movie, but there was a big plan for every soul, and the Supreme Beings made the decisions under the watchful eye of the Creator. It was all so complicated, and Levi was happy to be where he was in the overall scheme of things, just working his way up. His plans were set. Frank's destiny was in progress, and things were going to get interesting soon.

As they approached the barn, he could hear the sounds of horses whinnying at them. Levi had never been in the company of so many horses in his life, on Earth or on Plane 3. On Plane 3, they were mostly seen playing and frolicking in the huge green pastures created just for them. He would sit on hills and watch them in the distance, wondering what it would be like to ride one. But it was never a priority for him, because he just enjoyed the majesty of watching them from a distance. His recent encounter with the huge white horse had given him what he thought was a much better understanding of the creatures. He now wanted to know more about them.

They entered the barn through a huge, beautifully carved wooden door, again with the giant letter "K." This was completely unlike the experience he had had when they had first arrived on Earth and entered that old barn. No farmers with beers here. Was that classical music playing in the background? The horses were happy and clearly knew Frank well. As they walked down the line of neatly stacked hay and immaculate stalls, Frank proudly introduced Levi to each horse. This Frank guy didn't seem all that bad after all. He was thankful that Frank could not read his mind. Each horse was magnificent. Especially his beloved Magic, who he explained had been under the weather lately. Levi could tell that Frank was very worried about him. But he continued to walk down the line of stalls and brag about each horse as though they were his children. Frank had been married at one time, and his wife had died from cancer. It was tragic, and Levi wondered if Frank had given up on life a little after that and decided he didn't care about many things, about being a good guy. Maybe that was why he decided to take a lower road to wealth. But super wealthy he was. Every stall had a gold-plated plaque engraved with the name of the fabulous horse standing behind it.

It seemed like Frank had it all, but with failing health and business dealings that were constantly keeping him on the edge, Frank Kenning was a miserable and happy man all at the same time. He had a lovely woman in his life, wonderful animals, and a lifestyle that anyone would envy. He hid his problems well, but Levi knew that he was worried and desperate. Reaching out to the underworld for help was just another last-ditch attempt to make something happen in his life that was not going to work out well for him. The mysterious woman he had hired was a connection to evil. She was clearly someone who only Dani would be able to stop.

Speaking of Dani, Levi looked at his watch and realized that he needed to get to the car and get to the meeting place. He wasn't able to ascertain much about the home of Mr. Kenning from the brief meeting, but Dani had all the basic information she needed prior to the assignment, and Levi was only there to survey the big picture for her and to solidify a plan with Frank. It was so easy to do business on Earth when you had everything you needed at your disposal and you weren't using your own money. He knew this wasn't how it really worked on Earth, but it was exhilarating to be making a big real estate deal and rubbing elbows with the likes of Frank Kenning.

Mr. Kenning asked him if he wanted to meet at the site the next day or so to go over any last-minute details. Levi told him that would be great. They set a date for two days from then. Of course, there would be no need to visit the site with Frank, but Levi liked seeing him happy and excited to make this deal.

With that, they walked together to the house, and once inside, he again passed the photo on the table. As Levi turned, he saw a shadow pass along the landing at the top of the winding staircase. Was it Dani or Andromeda? He was anxious to get out of there. He had some questions for Dani. Once on the front landing, Levi looked for Dani but didn't see her. Instead, two large, hairy, black dogs came running, actually more like bouncing, around the side of the house. While they looked friendly, they immediately went to Frank's side and sat. They both fixed their eyes on Levi. As Levi slowly reached out to shake Frank's hand, he could swear he heard faint growling. Frank said something reassuring about not getting bitten. Levi smiled nervously and pulled back his hand. Levi was now somewhat wary of large, black, hairy dogs of any kind, Earthly or otherwise.

It was time to go.

Levi quickly got into the waiting car and instructed the driver go back to the designated spot where he would pick up Dani. The driver seemed completely confused by the whole episode, and Levi knew he wanted to ask some questions. Levi told him that Dani wanted to go for a walk because she had gotten carsick on the way up to the house. The driver seemed to fall for it, but Levi was anxious to get back to town or wherever Dani wanted to go and to move on and not have to answer any more Earthly questions.

About a mile from the estate, Levi could see Dani in the distance. She looked so out of place. As always. The driver's eyes lit up when her saw her, but he was smart not to make any comments, and she quickly got into the car. Levi was anxious to hear what she had to say, but talking about the plan in front of another human was not allowed, at least not verbally. They could do it telepathically, but it might seem strange for them to not talk at all during their drive. Some small talk would be in order.

Levi spoke first. "So, how was your walk, dear? Are you feeling better?"

As the cab slowly drove away, Dani looked at Levi and said, "I find the outdoors and the beautiful surroundings here to be very rejuvenating, *dear*."

With an emphasis on the "dear," he knew she was mocking him, and he could only take that to mean that she did not appreciate the sentiment and that he had better watch it. Tying himself to her in any way other than as Assistant was not going to work for her. On any level. She was a serious woman, and he would have to carefully choose his words and thoughts, which was something that he already knew. He wanted to kick himself for letting down his guard and thinking he could vary from the strict protocol that was within the scope of his job. He would not make the same mistake again. He should say nothing rather than say something stupid or inappropriate. He knew better. He would do better.

They needed to have a conversation about the day's events, and they would not be able to do that in the presence of a cab driver or anyone else. Dani quickly told the driver to take them to a nearby park just outside of town. She knew the place well, and there would be plenty of areas to be discrete and to be practically unnoticed.

It wasn't a long ride, and Levi was having a difficult time containing his thoughts. He knew she was in his head and that he couldn't do much about it. She didn't seem annoyed or upset about it, so he tried to be calm and wait for the next move. Plane 6 Elites had worked with many Assistants. Levi was sure that the whole telepathic communication thing had problems for both the Elites and the Assistants. Went with the territory. Even so, Levi wanted this to go well. He certainly didn't want to alienate the very person who might have to save his life. The fact that he could not read her mind was a bit disconcerting, but that was part of the deal. When you signed up to be an Assistant, you went with the program. Period. And Levi was actually okay with that. It did keep things simple and somewhat mysterious at the same time. The fact that he was fully protected and being looked out for at every turn made it all worth it.

They soon came to a stop, and Levi paid the driver, who by then was completely perplexed about the odd couple in his car. A gorgeous, tall woman and a plain, kind of short guy. He clearly thought it was weird. Levi also thought that the fact that the driver thought they were unmatched together would certainly mean that everyone else would, too. It wasn't going to be so easy integrating, especially with the potential of someone recognizing Dani. For the most part, she would be out of sight, but the fact that her guy Adam had actually already seen her meant that she was from the area. It was totally possible that another person would recognize her. But he would have to let her deal with it if it became a problem. He was sure that there was some Elite 6 form of memory erasing possible for someone who thought they had indeed seen a ghost. But clearly, she did not feel the need to do any erasing with Adam. Interesting. For now, he would just try to go with her flow.

# Chapter Twelve

It was a crisp and sunny late morning drive. They exited the cab, and Levi was relieved that they no longer had to keep up appearances for a driver who was having all kinds of bizarre thoughts. They walked far into the wooded area of the park. It was beautiful and serene. Levi could see himself living in an area like this if he were still on Earth. The afterlife wooded areas and parks were much different. It was hard to explain. They both had their own kind of charm, but in the afterlife, there was no danger lurking anywhere. On the Earth plane, even in a nice park, you never knew what might show up. Obviously, Levi was not at all worried. A giant Bigfoot with rabies could charge at them, and he knew he would be fine. He was also pretty sure that evil entities didn't hang out in the woods in broad daylight.

Dani headed for a bench that seemed to pop up out of nowhere. *Things were always popping up out of nowhere*, Levi thought to himself. He wondered quietly if Dani would mention the "dear" comment to him. She sat. He sat. He waited for her to speak. She seemed to be taking it all in, as if perhaps she had been there before, and there was some meaning tied to the place. He let her think. He was in no hurry to be scolded for being a moron.

Finally, she turned to him. "You know, Levi, life on Earth really is short. Humans do not grasp the precious nature of every single minute that they have here. I surely didn't. I loved my life, and I took for granted that I would live a certain way for a certain amount of time and that I was in control of what would happen to me, for the most part. Illnesses, demons, and accidents aside, it's what humans all want to believe. You and I are not of this world now. We understand this world, but be clear: we are not of it. We will be dealing with an entity that is also not of this world. Frank Kenning has entered into a remarkably dangerous partnership. He can be saved, and his soul can still ascend to Plane 3, but he will be subjected to Plane 2 scrutiny now, regardless of what happens here on Earth. Depending on how he deals with me, us, and the entity, these actions will determine how difficult that process will be for him. It can be fairly easy, as you know, or there can be dire consequences for Earthly indiscretions. Frank was a good man in the early years of his life. Loss can sometimes turn even the most kind and gentle person toward a life of greed and evil. While I would not classify Frank as evil, he has managed to seek out and find an intensely powerful demonic connection, which will do anything to capture and decimate his very soul. I will not allow that to happen. It really is a mess. The medium is looking for money, Frank is looking for a cure, and the entity is vying for a soul.

"I know that you were and are a good man, Levi. You must never lose sight of the fact that we are here to do a job. It's going to get ugly, and you'll need to be strong."

Levi was locked into position and stunned that Dani had even opened up to him at all, let alone in such a kind and loving way. He wasn't sure what to say, but he made an attempt.

"I am here to assist you in any way that you need me to. I appreciate your candor, and I am always open to learning to be better."

Dani shot him a look. "There will be little time for learning. You have been trained. Just go with your instincts, follow my lead, and try not to get killed."

There she was, the Dani he had come to fear and like all at the same time. It was clear she had a big heart, but the assignment took precedence over everything, and he needed to step up right now. He knew that she was being firm with him for his own good.

Dani asked, "What did you observe inside the house? What exactly did Andromeda do when she saw you?"

Levi thought for a moment. "It was almost as if she didn't really care about me at all. She did look at me as she ascended the staircase but then turned and walked on. She didn't behave as though I was any kind of threat."

"That is because you are not a threat," Dani remarked with calm assurance. "She senses that we're here. That I'm here. She knows that it's possible that her plan may be interrupted, and she has already started her poison potion protocol on Frank. She will attempt to undermine anything that we might do to save his soul. She also knows the approximate death time and date for Frank, which is something she did not share with her murdering cohorts. If that time is missed, the entity that she conjures could potentially acquire his soul. What color were her eyes?"

Levi thought for a moment, not wanting to get it wrong. "Pulsing greenish-yellow."

"This will be a relatively easy entity to deal with. Dangerous but stupid," she said with a roll of her eyes. "We must get Frank to the place of his destiny death at the exact time that it should naturally occur, as you know. The house is a fortress to humans, but it is not impermeable to the likes of evil entities from beyond. It is possible that if they perceive our threat to be too great, they will bring in reinforcements. We will act quickly, driving the one demon away."

With that, the hair on Levi's neck stood up. More than one evil entity? Maybe the Zengats wouldn't be able to fight off multiple demons. Maybe he had gotten himself into something even more dangerous than his training had indicated. But he didn't have a choice at this point. Here he was, and he would put his trust in the only Plane 6 Elite around to get him through it all. Alive. Well, dead...

They had less than three Earth hours left to get Frank on his way to the afterlife. It seemed like a long time, but there was much to do. Levi knew that this confrontation with evil would be nothing like the stupid, half-drunk men in the barn. That was child's play compared to this.

Dani began to lay out their plan of attack. First, Levi would confirm his meeting with Frank at the new building site, a meeting that would never take place. They knew that

Charlotte would be arriving at the house at a certain time as well, so Frank would be there as scheduled to wait for her. Dani and Levi would be waiting at the house prior to Frank's death due date and hour. Levi would enter the property through a back gate that Dani would leave open for him. The guard dogs would be an issue for Levi, so Dani would ensure that they were preoccupied prior to the plan being put into action. Dani knew that the medium would be caught off-guard, even though she knew Dani was nearby. Even if she were possessed, Dani could work her stealth magic and maneuver around her and her evil personal guest or guests.

Dani was aware that because Andromeda knew there was an Elite being in the midst, she would have to step up her plan to get Frank to sign papers, and the entity that she was hosting made it clear that it wanted Frank's soul. Andromeda had told Felipe that there was a change of plans. They would have to move quickly to get the papers signed, and she would have to increase the potion strength to cause Frank to lose his inhibitions enough to sign those papers. Felipe wondered about the sudden change in plans, but the medium was not about to explain that there could be interference from another being from the other side that could potentially blow the whole plan. Nobody would believe that story.

Levi would take a position near the barn and wait for Dani to make her move on the medium. If things went as planned, there would be a short confrontation, and the medium would back off and leave the premises. If she decided to take Dani on and try to keep Frank alive, or dead based on her timeframe, well, the fur was going to fly. Levi was to stay put in the barn and out of sight. Levi knew that Magic was going to die in the midst of everything and that his death was on schedule. Frank's late wife, Kristen, would be there to pass the horse over, and that was not of any concern to Levi or Dani. It would happen no matter what went on with Frank. Frank was to pass over with Dani. That was the agreement. He would be confused at first, but there was a plan to reunite him with Magic and his family members as soon as possible. Frank's death would take place in his barn. He would hopefully die of a sudden and massive heart attack, and that would be the end of that story. His story on Earth.

Felipe and Andromeda had other ideas. During the last several weeks, Andromeda, who appeared harmless to Frank, and very unattractive by Levi's standards, was giving Frank potions that basically did nothing to either cure or stall his illness; however, it was causing him to become disoriented at times and not altogether clearheaded, which was exactly what they wanted to get him to sign some important paperwork before they killed him. The document would give all power to Felipe regarding the drug business, not to mention some highly valuable real estate holdings. Felipe would have to take care of Richard sooner than later. He had set off to make that accident happen. He would check in after Frank was dead and papers were signed.

Frank really believed that he was going to live. To be cured. It was all a lie, and Frank had fallen for it. He thought that he would be saved by some miracle potion and that he would in turn simply give Felipe a lot of money. Andromeda was counting on the big score to change her miserable life. People like Andromeda generally didn't make a lot of money, and she knew she had hit the big time with this client. She would pull out all the stops to get rich, even enlist the help of an entity that was dangerous and elusive. Even to her. She didn't care if Frank's soul went to hell. That was just part of the medium-entity contract, so to speak. She wanted money, and the entity wanted a soul.

Felipe would have to share the spoils with her and CJ. He surely didn't want to risk retribution from CJ or his evil business associate, Andromeda. He had no idea what they might be capable of, and he didn't want to find out.

Frank was unaware of what he was really dealing with. He had approached a soothsayer via a friend of his and was told that this person could help him in ways that no one else could. In a desperate attempt to prolong and save his life, he had opened himself up to all kinds of unsavory characters, not the least of which was Felipe, his somewhat trusted associate, and while demons must be summoned by a particular type of human, Frank had no clue how that worked. He hadn't wanted to know about the demon part of the deal. By making the mistake of getting involved with these people, he had created the potential for his passing to be incredibly difficult and traumatizing. All unnecessary. His natural death was destined to be calm and sudden, like so many heart attacks could be. It is never a good thing on Earth to die and suffer a great deal doing it, but Frank was unwittingly putting himself at risk for just that. He was the one interfering with his destiny, a destiny that was approaching the end game.

Dani explained to Levi what would happen if Andromeda brought in reinforcements, meaning more than one entity. They would also have to work around the arrival of Charlotte. It was getting a bit complicated, for sure. Levi's part was set in stone. He would do his job well, and they would have a successful transition. He hoped. Dani did not get into the details about what her actions might be. That was all dependent on the medium and who she conjured up to help her. Dani was aware that Andromeda knew she was going to be dealing with an Elite. Even unsavory humans like her understood that there were super beings from the other side just waiting to interfere with their Earthly plans. While Andromeda had some fairly impressive abilities on Earth, she was no match for an Elite, which is why she conjured help from Plane 1. And although she was overly confident in her abilities, even with help from Plane 1, she would not be able to transition a human soul from earth to anywhere. She was human, and her goal was money. Pure and simple.

The entities from Plane 1 were not intelligent beings. They were a subspecies group that only existed at the will of the Creator for the purposes of conflict and fear. Something that did not exist on the other planes. It was an unfortunate necessity to keep the Universe balanced. This nasty group was always trying to add to its numbers, thinking that at some point they would rule the world, which could not have been further from the truth. The checks and balances of the Universe were always in motion. When Plane 1 beings were involved, it always got messy, but they would never rule anything. They could only cause trouble. And they were getting good at it.

# Chapter Thirteen

It was getting close to Frank's destined death. The morning he was supposed to die, he woke up tired and a bit hazy. As he slowly walked down the winding staircase to the main floor, he looked over the beautiful home he had created and thought about how truly lucky he was. What would happen to this place after he was gone? He had left most of it to Charlotte in his will, the drug business to Richard (in a separate agreement), and the rest to charity. He felt good about those decisions. But it wasn't something he was ready to deal with. His life had evolved so much in the last several months, and Charlotte had changed everything for him. He was a different man now; he was a new version of the old him. The good guy. He had it all, and he knew that the drug business was not a positive thing. It had taken him down an ugly path, and he was anxious to be rid of the whole thing. He wanted to get on with his wonderful life with Charlotte. He felt a renewed sense of wonder at all that he had created. It was like a new start, in a way. He had always loved animals, but they had taken on an even more important role in his life. They were family. He adored his dogs and his beloved Magic. He wished that he could live forever.

As he entered the massive kitchen and looked out onto the huge expanse of his backyard, he thought about the regrets in his life. There were many. Most were related to the loss of his wife and some serious estrangements from his other family members due to a life of excess and self-indulgence. And the drug business, of course. One regret that always remained uniquely difficult for him to deal with was the death of the young woman whom he had given one of Magic's babies to, Danielle. The whole thing was a horrible memory. Even now, it seemed like yesterday.

She was so happy the day Cole was delivered to her home, and Frank was suddenly caught in a moment of joy that he had not felt in years, pure joy at the look on her face when she saw the beautiful creature step off the trailer. He would never forget it, and he would never forget her. Her fiancé Adam was his veterinarian, and they had all been close and worked together so well. Years later, when Cole died, it was devastating for her and for Frank. Dani continued to work for him, and even though the sadness was sometimes palpable, Frank knew that her future would become brighter. He would see to that. She had done a great job for his company. He had big plans for her.

They had talked about another horse in her future eventually, and Dani was hoping that with her impending wedding and life with Adam, things would get better. She was smart, funny, and an up-and-coming potential real estate mogul. He could tell. He had hired her soon after she acquired her license. She was just beginning her career with Frank's company when a not-so-chance encounter with a thief and murderer cut her life short. No one could have seen it coming. At least, that was what Frank liked to tell himself. He knew that it was drug-related. He knew that because of him, she was dead. It had all gone terribly wrong. He had agreed to list a fellow drug dealer's estate, and in exchange, they would launder some money through the sale. Simple, Frank thought. He had done it a hundred times before. Unfortunately, he and Richard had not done their homework on this guy. Felipe said that he was solid and not to worry. They could trust him. Felipe had never led Frank astray before, so he went along with the deal, which involved the usual money laundering exercise. In exchange for commissions, there would be a large shipment of Frank's special drug delivered after the sale. What Frank didn't know was that Felipe had a side deal going at the same time with this client, and he had made some promises that he couldn't keep.

The owner of the home decided to make a big and ugly statement to Frank and his crew, and he specifically asked that Frank's new protege, Dani, list the house. He had been swindled by Felipe, and he took his revenge on Frank by killing Dani. It was all so senseless. Frank would never know that Felipe had everything to do with it. He only knew that the drug business had created the situation, and that situation had taken Dani.

He turned to the long, black, marble counter, and the cup of dark-red tea was waiting for him, like it was every morning. As he reached for the cup, he wondered if he was really feeling any better. This old woman had come to live at the house weeks ago and was supposed to be slowing the disease process and eventually eliminating it altogether with her strange brew. Why didn't he feel better? He was beginning to have bouts of dizziness and forgetfulness, all signs that his doctors had warned him about.

Was he being played? Was this really a cure for his illness? He was tired and didn't even want to think about it right now. She was a strange old woman, and he didn't like having her in the house. His drug-dealing partner Felipe had recommended her, and Frank was desperately in need of a cure. He could feel the effects of the illness beginning to take hold, and he wanted it to stop. It all seemed so crazy now, using some bizarre woman with a mysterious potion to heal him. He was spending a lot of money and wasn't even sure it was working.

Where was Andromeda, anyway? She was usually creeping around someplace. It might have been at that very moment that he decided she had to go. Potion and all. He didn't bother to drink the tea and went to the faucet to get a drink of water. Something was off. He was off.

As he walked toward the back door, he had to catch himself, because he felt faint. What was happening? Where were his dogs? They would always greet him at the door in the morning, ready to walk with him to the barn. He stopped and stood for a moment and realized that the old woman was standing right behind him. Startled, he turned to see what he thought were her eyes turning a strange shade of yellow. Then greenish. Was he losing it? She put her hand on his shoulder and calmly asked him a question.

"Mr. Kenning, are you not going to drink your tea this morning? You really should, and remember the papers that you need to sign today."

Papers? He was meeting Levi at the project tomorrow to sign papers. What was she talking about? His mind was spinning suddenly, and all he wanted to do was go to the barn and see his horses. See his Magic. He continued out the door, with the old woman following close behind.

Frank headed for the barn, and Levi had entered the property and was also heading for the barn, cautiously avoiding Frank's line of sight. Levi could see that Frank was moving slowly and rubbing his eyes. He could also see the Andromeda following close behind, waving a handful of papers at him. As destiny would have it, Levi could see a car arriving at the gate. That would be Charlotte. Levi knew that she would be in for a shock if things got dicey. No way to prevent that. It was something that Dani would ultimately handle.

Levi entered the barn and could see that Magic was not standing at the front of his stall or whinnying. Frank's dead wife, Kristen, was bending down next to the horse, who was also clearly dead or very close to it. It was awful and comforting at the same time to see the majestic horse in distress and to know that he would be happily on his way to a wonderful afterlife. Kristen briefly acknowledged Levi, and that was the end of that interaction. They both knew what was about to go down, and the sooner it was over with, the better.

Levi could see Dani coming around the side of the house. As Frank walked toward the barn, the old woman turned to see Dani and squared off with her. There was no look of surprise from the woman, almost as if she expected to see a Plane 6 Elite at some point.

He waited and could only watch from a distance as the woman faced Dani. What a sight it was! The two women could not be more different.

He watched Frank saunter toward the open barn door, completely unaware of what was happening behind him, looking around and wondering where his dogs were. In a raspy voice, he called out for them and continued toward the barn. *Keep moving, Frank*, Levi thought, *keep moving, and don't look back.*

He would be in for a different kind of shock when he reached the barn. During the night, his beloved horse Magic had begun his path to death due to a mysterious blood disorder and was lying still in his stall. Levi wasn't sure he could deal with another horse tragedy. He was glad that he was not an animal transition provider. He thought of his dog Sparky and how heart-wrenching it would be for his family when he passed.

This animal death would be an important part of Frank's destined heart attack. Kristen waited patiently with Magic, who was laying still, until Frank could experience his own demise.

It was coming to a head, all at the same time. The old woman's ploy to get Frank to sign everything over to his supposed friend, the Colombian, was going sideways. Instead of Dani having to step in and obliterate the demon to stop the signing of the agreement, Frank had made his own decision, had signed nothing over to anyone, and was on his way to his timely death. The sight of Dani had kept the woman from interrupting Frank's walk to the barn, and she waved the papers with frustration.

Somewhere in the city, Felipe was putting his plan together to kill Richard, not knowing that the shit was about to hit the fan back at the estate. Without the papers signed, the drug business would not be his directly, and all of the formulas would disappear. Frank and Richard had made sure of that. If anything happened to them, there was a plan in place for everything to be destroyed. Formulas, all drug business-related information, all of it. Like it had never existed. Frank and Richard did not want anything to come back and haunt their families. Felipe would be left with nothing.

Seeing his beloved horse dead would be a shock, and Levi was not looking forward to Frank having to experience that. The good news was that he would soon be reunited with Magic, and all would be as it should be.

His dogs, who were now looking for Frank, had been distracted by a rabbit that had breached the fencing. They now came running around the side of the house. They were confused and started to growl loudly at the two women, who were obviously engaged in some sort of conflict. Andromeda put a quick spell of some kind on them, and they both dropped to the ground as though they had been shot. In fact, they were simply stunned and would not be involved in the action that was about to take place.

At that moment, Frank turned to see the odd group that was now assembled in his back yard. Was he hallucinating, or were his dogs dead? He could see two women in the distance. He knew the old woman, but was that Danielle? Was it her? His mind was on overload.

Frank took a couple of steps towards the two women, and his eyes met Dani's. He knew it was her. At that intense moment, she felt his remorse and sadness about what had happened to her.

But now was not the time for a reunion. Frank stopped in his tracks, and Dani directed him to the barn. He was so confused, but he did as he was told. By a dead woman.

Dani and the demon turned to face each other. Andromeda reached out towards Dani, and with a wave of her hand, Dani summoned three Zengats, who appeared out of nowhere and surrounded the old woman. The demon within the woman had never seen such creatures and was taken aback. Demon-possessed Andromeda bared her ugly teeth at Dani, the Zengats bared theirs, and it was clear that there was no chance that she would win this battle.

Suddenly, it was as though the woman transformed into an ugly, greenish reptilian monster. Dani moved away from the four growling creatures, and her aura changed. She began to glow. Her eyes were a bright shade of purple, pulsing and directed at the thrashing entity.

The three Zengats attacked, and a swirling mass of hair and green flesh filled the air.

A strange concoction of what could only be called goo oozed around the fighting foursome's feet. Papers were flying everywhere, and the demon's eyes were flashing red with anger and fear. Andromeda was for all intents and purposes gone. The demon had completely taken her over and was trying to take on Dani and the Zengats. Big mistake. The goo was becoming purplish in color, and the Zengats were not liking it one bit. Jumping out of the muck and growling loudly at the angry entity, they watched as the muck began to swallow it up until it disappeared into a mass of greenish black and melted into the grass below. Levi was watching and holding his breath. He would have to get Frank to his death time with or without Dani now. It was all happening so fast; however, it appeared that Dani and the Zengats had things under control. He watched as the wicked thing disappeared into the ground, reminiscent of a popular fairy tale ending. He didn't have time to be fearful or upset. He was now focused on Frank.

Frank had entered the barn, completely unaware of the crazy scene behind him.

Levi was watching the clock. It was getting close to his time.

Dani stood and watched as the screaming demon disappeared. The Zengats shook off their goo-laden paws and stood next to Dani. That was done. This wicked creature had not helped Frank's partner to acquire everything that Frank owned, and she clearly had not brought enough reinforcements.

As it turned out, this was a relatively easy demon to deal with. It was a three-Zengat process, but Dani knew that one or two would have gotten it done. When demons inhabit a human body, they become vulnerable to Earthly death. Not the smartest beings in the Universe, they still needed to figure out how to stay alive long enough to accomplish their evil intentions. Dani knew that the word would get out to the Plane 1 crowd, and they would soon be working hard to figure out new and treacherous ways to deal with the Elites who would surely come to stop them in the future.

It didn't matter now. Frank was on his way to a better existence, to a true place of love and acceptance. His partner, Richard, would experience the same thing in the not-too-distant future. He would stay in the drug game a little too long after Frank's death and would pay a heavy price. Felipe's plan for Richard to die in an accident would not work out. Richard would survive the crash. Felipe would have to try to make a different deal with CJ, which would eventually lead to his own untimely and ruthless demise.

# Chapter Fourteen

The wicked witch was dead and gone. Dani released her hounds back to where they had come from and looked at the leftover carnage surrounding her. Charlotte would soon encounter the bizarre scene. Dani eventually would have to put a spell of sorts on Charlotte, wake up the dogs, and clear away the residue left by the melting incident. Charlotte wouldn't remember anything she had seen in the yard, once she arrived at the entrance to the barn.

Dani was ready to let go of her negative feelings towards Frank. She understood that his lifestyle had paved the way for her early death, in a way, but it was all meant to be. Her destiny. He had not wanted her to die.

Levi had watched the dog and demon show from the barn. It was scary and exhilarating all at the same time. He knew Dani would make short work of her, and he was surprised that it took three Zengats to get the job done. The demon was pretty damn scary, and Levi was amazed that he was able to take it all in and not faint in the process. He also knew that this was just the beginning of his adventures as an Assistant and that things could and would get a lot hairier in the future.

Frank had entered the barn. The time was near. As he walked forward, he wondered why Magic had not come to the front of the stall to greet him like he always did. He could hear the other horses moving around in an agitated manner, and he was confused as to what was going on. He looked around and saw nothing out of the ordinary in the barn, unlike the bizarre hallucination he had just experienced in the backyard. His head was spinning as he tried to make sense of it all. He thought he could hear Charlotte calling out to him in the distance.

Levi remained hidden. Frank moved closer to the stall of his beloved horse. It was awful to see the look on Frank's face as he leaned over the gate to see his best friend lying dead. Tears ran down his face as he held on tight to steady himself. He was heartbroken, literally.

Dani entered the barn from the yard ahead of Charlotte, who did not see her, and waited quietly for the few seconds it would take for Frank to die.

Levi looked over at Kristen, who was quietly standing guard over Frank's beloved horse. Their eyes met in sweet sorrow.

Frank turned to see Dani approaching him. As though it wasn't at all strange to see her, he simply said, "I've lost my Magic, Danielle."

He put his hand on his heart, and almost in slow motion, he crumpled to the floor.

He looked upward for a few seconds and soon closed his eyes, as though falling asleep.

Levi hadn't been sure how he would feel in this moment, actually watching someone die. He had now seen two horses die, one brought back to life, an old demon obliterated by beasts from heaven, and now a human death.

As Frank lay motionless on the floor in the aisle of the barn, there was silence. Even the horses were soundless. The trauma and drama that had unfolded in front of them had left them stunned and unsure of what was next.

Frank was gone. Magic was gone.

Charlotte was now making her way to the barn in search of Frank. She assumed that he would be there as usual, tending to his animals. What she had seen when she left the kitchen was startling, and she was confused and scared. His two dogs were lying silently on the ground, dead. Or so she thought. She had quickly run to them and realized that they were still breathing. Where was Frank? What was going on?

As Charlotte looked toward the barn, she realized that something was wrong. It was all wrong. The dogs would normally be with Frank in the barn. What was wrong with them? She began to panic.

Dani knelt down next to Frank. His energy began to fill the barn. His aura was beautiful as it swirled around him. The horses in the barn were scared, and they exited their stalls and then ran into the pastures.

Charlotte could see the horses panicking and exiting the barn in all directions. She had to find out what was happening. Afraid but determined, she started to run to the barn, calling out Frank's name.

Frank's soul was now standing next to Dani. His Magic was standing in front of him.

It all happened in seconds.

Dani looked at Levi and told him telepathically to meet her, Magic, and Kristen at the place where they would all three ascend.

Frank's soul was ready to make its transition. Levi, Magic, and Kristen soon disappeared. Frank could not see or feel anything around him now, only Dani. He was calm. There were no words spoken, and the two of them passed through the barn into a space of whirling colors.

By the time Charlotte reached the barn, it was over. She saw Frank on the floor and ran to him. With tears running down her cheeks, she hugged his lifeless body and kissed him one last time. What had happened? He was on his way to being healed. How could this be? As she stood to call an ambulance, she leaned against Magic's stall, only to realize that he too was dead. She was barely able to make the call before she too crumpled to the ground, sobbing.

As she sat on the floor in disbelief, his dogs Benny and Bart entered the barn and immediately went to Frank's side and laid down. It was quiet. She had almost forgotten about the strange woman who had been living in the house and half expected her to show up in the barn. But she was nowhere to be seen.

Soon, sirens could be heard in the distance as Charlotte sat with Frank and his dogs in somber sadness.

Life at the estate would never be the same. Charlotte would be taken care of, as well as his horses and dogs. Frank had made sure of that. Soon, there would be lots of people walking around the property. Some of Frank's police buddies, friends, and numerous business associates, would be stunned and worried that their cash cow was gone. The drug business would be changed in ways that they knew were going to make it difficult to continue on and to be effective and lucrative. Richard's life would be in turmoil, and he would be worried that the police who were not drug business-friendly would soon be on his trail without the careful and watchful eye of Frank.

Word spread quickly about Frank's death at the Kenning estate. His beloved horses would stay where they were in the loving care of his new love, Charlotte. The loss of Magic would be noted in the breeding world. He had sired amazing animals and would be missed, even by people who had never had the pleasure of being in his majestic presence.

It was all behind Frank now. It was all over.

The finality and quickness of actual death on Earth was difficult for people to comprehend.

For Frank, it was a few seconds in time.

While Frank had limited family and true friends, he would be missed. Greed and loneliness had taken its toll, and he was not the man he had wanted to be for a large part of his life, but there was a tendency for people to think about the good things, especially when they had no clue about all of the bad.

Frank had made sure that his closest friends and family knew nothing about his illegal and immoral business.

He had made so many mistakes, so many poor decisions.

Soon after he hit the floor, he was already leaving his body and walking through a strange and wonderful light show of brilliant colors swirling around him with Dani.

Was that Magic in the distance? He moved more quickly now. Was he walking or floating? He wasn't sure. All he cared about was getting to his horse, touching him, and feeling that precious moment of love and understanding. Nothing else seemed to matter now. Nothing. He didn't care where he was, he didn't feel any pain, and he was compelled to move forward. As he came closer to his beloved horse, he could see another figure standing close by. She was familiar. Seeing her with his horse brought back a flood of memories. Was that her? Was that his wife Kristen? A rush of pure love ran through him like a bolt of lightning. Magic began to move towards him, and he soon felt the familiar touch of his velvet coat and the warmth that emanated from his big, dark eyes. It was as though they had been apart for a lifetime, and it had only been minutes in Earth time. But it was all different now. They were in an unfamiliar place. He was suddenly overwhelmed with happiness and relief.

Dani stepped in front of him. He was speechless. She had saved him somehow. His thoughts were running wild. He tried to understand everything, but he struggled to put the pieces together. It was all so overwhelming.

Dani finally spoke. "Frank, you are heading home. This is the beginning of that journey. Magic, Kristen, and anyone or any animal you have ever cared for who has passed will be waiting for you very soon.

"You are in transition from the Earth plane to the afterlife. There is a process that will prepare you for your eternal life. You will have choices to make, and in time, all things will become clear, and you will have the opportunity to enjoy your existence without pain, regret, or worry.

"I must leave you now. Magic will be fine, and you will soon be with him again. There is someone who is waiting to reunite with him now. I promise I will watch over him until you are ready."

Frank was still stunned but taking it all in. He now knew that he was dead. It was amazing. He had no sense of longing or sadness for his dogs, horses, Charlotte, or anything else on Earth. Seeing Magic gave him comfort and the sense that he would see them all again. Knowing that took any anxiety away.

He looked at Dani and felt a wave of appreciation and forgiveness. Forgiveness from her.

He knew that something bad connecting him to her had taken place and that the powerful feelings attached to her would be something he only hoped he would eventually understand. His memory was fading, and he was so wrapped up in the moment he could hardly speak. But he was able to say to her with tears in his eyes, "I hope to see you again. Thank you."

Another figure entered the space of light and color and gently guided him away. Dani stood and watched as the man who had been involved in her very murder went to be absolved and forever changed.

Levi was petting the huge, black horse and taking it all in. This was definitely the good part of the assignment. He waited for Dani to walk over to him but was surprised when she seemed to disappear. It was quiet, and as he stood next to Magic, he felt a warm breeze pass through the space that they now occupied. He knew that the return was easy and gentle. This was also a new experience. He was told by The Ancients to go with the flow of the ascension process and enjoy. The fog and colors now swirled slowly around them, and he soon saw a clearing where the familiar and lush landscape of the afterlife loomed in the distance. Was that Dani? Where was Kristen?

Was that another black horse? Of course, it was Cole, the very horse that she had acquired from Frank Kenning. Magic's baby.

Before Levi could have another thought, the huge beast beside him began to run toward the beautiful horse in the distance. Dani moved away, and together, the two horses galloped off into the countryside of green and rolling pastures. Levi had seen many horses in the afterlife, but this duo was something special. He had become fond of horses and had a new appreciation of their connection to humans and how important they were in the fabric of life on Earth and beyond.

He was back. Just like that. The afterlife did not mess around. Things happened quickly. Perfectly. He had learned a lot on his journey to Earth. He had grown in ways he never could have imagined. He had bonded with a Plane 6 Elite, not something he ever dreamed was possible. He had taken a chance and trusted her with his life. She had taken care of him. He felt empowered, and yet he was now unsure that he actually wanted to be a Plane 6 Elite. He fully enjoyed being her partner. He liked his role as Assistant, and he really liked the Zengats, even though he knew they would never have any kind of normal bond. He respected the fact that they were simply pure protection. Nothing complicated. They saved and occasionally took lives, all in the name of good. Something he might have to deal with again in the near future.

He knew there would be a debriefing regarding the recovery. He looked forward to it. He wondered how much of the "un-recovery" activity would be presented, if any. He would never snitch on Dani. He owed her much more than his safe journey to Earth and back. He respected her immensely, and he knew that after the download, he might never see her again.

That was the way. Different recoveries, different Assistants. That was his understanding. He would move forward and work with whomever he was paired with.

He was emotionally spent. He wasn't physically tired, just full of thoughts and energy that needed to subside. There were places in the afterlife for that. On Earth, they would be called spas. He was anxious to see his son and feel the calm associated with general life on Plane 3.

He wondered how Dani was doing. It had been a crazy and outrageous journey for her. Not only confronting the man who played a part in her death but also seeing her beloved Adam again must have been somewhat painful. But Levi felt that she would be fine. She was the strongest, most self-assured person he had ever met. He had nothing but admiration and respect for her.

As he turned to head to his familiar surroundings, he looked back to see Dani standing on a small hill overlooking the pasture that Magic and Cole ran and played in. There were other horses there with them. It was a wonderful feeling. There was a lot of that in the afterlife.

Levi had survived his first Class X Recovery.

He knew that it would not be long before he would be off again to Earth and to another adventure. He had been terrified at times—and also had never felt more alive.

He couldn't wait to do it again.

# Chapter Fifteen

Felipe found out like everyone else—via the local news —that Frank had died of a heart attack in his barn. He had unfinished business with Richard, but he needed to get the signed paperwork before Richard got his hands on it.

He would have to be careful in the way he collected the paperwork that he thought had been signed. He would have to make his way to the house, meet with the medium, and get what he needed. He knew that the place would be crawling with people and maybe some reporters. He had to go now while things were in disarray. Charlotte would not get what was going on, and he could get in and out. His plan to get rid of Richard had failed. That would be the next thing on his agenda. As long as the papers were signed, he would figure it out.

He hurried to Frank's estate and talked his way in, saying that he was one of Frank's relatives.

The police had not yet arrived, and he was able to walk right into the house where Charlotte was sitting on the couch in the living room with Frank's two huge dogs parked on either side of her. They saw him and immediately began to growl. Lucky for him, they listened to Charlotte. She knew he was one of Frank's business associates. Felipe acted as sad and distressed as he possibly could and gave his condolences to Charlotte, careful not to get too close to her.

He knew that the dogs were not friendly, and he didn't want to be attacked. No telling what they might do without Frank around to stop them.

He had to act fast and get out of there. So he told her he was going to pick up some paperwork that Frank was leaving for him in the kitchen, and he would just go and pick that up, if that was okay. Charlotte was a mess, and the dogs were not going to stop growling. She waved him on, not realizing what he was up to, of course.

As he entered the kitchen, he looked for the papers and for Andromeda, who didn't seem to be anywhere in sight. Perhaps she had done her job and left? He didn't see any papers on the counter, and he started to feel like something had not gone as planned. As he looked around the kitchen, he looked out the window and saw several white pieces of paper strewn across the lawn.

That was odd. He decided to go and take a look. As he approached one of the pages, he could see paramedics and some other people leaving the barn. He soon realized that the papers were his contract and they had not been signed. He sidestepped a puddle of odd-looking residue and proceeded to gather the papers. Were those giant dog footprints? He would have to find Andromeda and get to the bottom of it all.

It was going to get complicated, and he would set his sights on Richard, knowing that he would be taking over the drug business now. With Frank out of the way, it might be easier to get what he wanted. Time would tell. He gathered up the mangled papers.

He decided to leave quietly and quickly, bypassing Charlotte and her new guardians, and connect with CJ, who surely knew where the old woman was. He wanted to find out what had happened and put a new plan into action. This wasn't over.

# Home

Dani looked on as the two horses played together in the pasture like they had never been apart. She could stand and watch forever. She would enjoy spending time with Cole and Magic, as she did with all her animal friends.

Frank was off to be indoctrinated, and he would soon reunite with his wife, friends, and his beloved Magic. He wasn't a bad man. He had just followed his worst ambitions for a time. In his coming afterlife experience, like Dani, he too would discover who Dani's killer was. All in due time. And he and Dani would bond and become good friends.

As she walked away and back to her life as an Elite being, she thought of Adam. She knew that he had seen her. It must have been so strange and unbelievable to him. She was counting on it. She didn't need him pondering the idea that she was lurking around someplace, just waiting to materialize.

Adam's time would come. They would be together again. His destiny was set. She would be there to greet him when he passed over. Only time and other Class X Recoveries would determine if she would encounter him again on the Earth plane.

She would go through the debriefing process and probably have to explain the white horse scenario. Perhaps not. No one had died during that side event, and she had left things much better than she had found them.

She thought about Levi. For her, this was a relatively easy transition. She knew he would have a lot to think about. She liked him. A lot. She knew that when the time came again, she would ask specifically for him to be her Assistant. The transitions would get more intense and dangerous. She knew she could count on him and felt that Levi was the man for the next job.

Dani took one last look at the two horses, now walking close together, and wondered about her next assignment. A Plane 6 Elite had gone rogue during a Class X Recovery. It was someone whom she knew. It would be a complicated situation. Just her style. She headed to the palace, feeling good about her afterlife existence and what was ahead. It was good to be home.

Made in the USA
Columbia, SC
14 November 2018